## "Would you consider... being the nanny?"

"I don't have much experience," Katie said.

"I've got some flexibility in my schedule, and the kids are gone half the day at school, so it won't be much time. I know they can be...overwhelming sometimes. Especially when they're armed with finger paint and a hose." He grinned.

Sam's smile was a little lopsided, with a slight dimple in his left cheek. She liked his smile. Liked it a lot. Wouldn't mind seeing it more often. And if he was going to be around to help with the kids... Was she seriously considering this job?

Her gaze traveled again to Libby, then to Henry, dwarfed by an oversize chair in the living room.

A feeling tugged at something deep inside of Katie, something she hadn't even been sure existed until she'd walked into this house and met these children. This man.

"Okay," she said. "I'll do it."

\* \* \*

**The Barlow Brothers:**
Nothing tames a Southern man
faster... than true love!

# WINNING THE NANNY'S HEART

BY
SHIRLEY JUMP

MILLS & BOON

First Published in Great Britain 2017
By Mills & Boon, an imprint of HarperCollins*Publishers*
1 London Bridge Street, London, SE1 9GF

© 2016 Shirley Kawa-Jump, LLC

ISBN: 978-0-263-92269-1

23-0117

Our policy is to use papers that are natural, renewable and recyclable products and made from wood grown in sustainable forests. The logging and manufacturing processes conform to the legal environmental regulations of the country of origin.

Printed and bound in Spain
by CPI, Barcelona

*New York Times* and *USA TODAY* bestselling author **Shirley Jump** spends her days writing romance so she can avoid the towering stack of dirty dishes, eat copious amounts of chocolate and reward herself with trips to the mall. Visit her website at www.shirleyjump.com for author news and a booklist, and follow her at Facebook.com/shirleyjump.author for giveaways and deep discussions about important things like chocolate and shoes.

To my awesome, supersmart editor Susan Litman,
who has made every one of The Barlow Brothers
books better and stronger.
Working with her has been an honor and a pleasure.

# Chapter One

The first time Katie Williams ran away from home, she was eight years old.

She packed her Barbie backpack with a clean T-shirt, a handful of granola bars and three stuffed animals (because she couldn't possibly choose between Rabbit, Harvey and Willard), then set out into the world. Well, not the world, really, just the end of Seventh Street, where the alley met the back of the park. She'd settled into the dark, tight space under the stairs for the slide, and told herself she wasn't scared.

Her brother, Colton, found her an hour later, hungry and weepy and cold. "I was gonna make pancakes for breakfast tomorrow, Piglet," he'd said, as if it were just another ordinary Tuesday. "And nobody wants to miss out on pancakes." He wrapped her in the thick fleeced comfort of his sweatshirt, then carried her home piggyback. While he walked, his back hunched under her weight, he told her a story about a brave princess who lived in a castle high on a hill, with an ogre for a friend. Colton had carried her straight to her room, deposited Katie in her squeaky twin bed and bundled her under the thin blankets. He paused, then let out a sigh.

*She did it again*, Colton had said.

It wasn't even a question. Katie nodded, afraid to say the words out loud. To tell her brother how their mother had lashed out at Katie again, for a sin no more egregious than asking if there was anything for supper. In those days, their mother drank more than she ate, and for whatever reason, had taken her anger out on Katie more than Colton.

Colton had given her a nod of understanding, a hug and a whisper in her ear, *You're a good kid. Don't ever forget that*. He'd talked to her until her tears dried up and then he'd tucked her into her bed, and left her with a sandwich he'd sneaked out of the kitchen.

She supposed it was kind of ironic that almost twenty years later, she was running away from home again, but this time *toward* her brother. And once again, he didn't ask a single question when she showed up on his doorstep late in the afternoon in a tiny quaint town in North Carolina.

"Hey," she said, when she walked into the Stone Gap Fire Department and found Colton standing by Engine No. 1, polishing the chrome. "I'm here."

He stopped working, tossed the rag onto the counter and grinned at her. "Hey yourself, Piglet." She'd never escaped his childhood nickname for her, but that was okay. "'Bout time you showed up."

She propped a fist on her hip and gave her six-foot-two brother a well-practiced look of annoyance. He was seven inches taller than her and looked ten times stronger in his dark blue uniform. But that didn't stop her from teasing him. "Just because you call and invite me to come visit you doesn't mean I'm going to rush on down here."

"I don't know why not. Seeing as how I'm your favorite person and all." His grin widened and he stepped forward, opening his arms and dragging her into a hug before she could protest. "Even if you are my annoying little sister."

Katie drew back and squared her shoulders. She could have leaned into Colton's hug forever, but if she did that, she was afraid the fragile hold she had on her emotions would crumble, and then she'd be a sobbing mess. If there was one thing Katie didn't do, it was cave to emotions. She hadn't gotten to be a partner at one of the largest accounting firms in Atlanta by acting weak. And she wasn't going to get through the next couple weeks without staying strong.

After that, she should be fine. Or at least that was what she had told herself the whole way here. Two weeks, she'd decided, was long enough to find a new job, a new life, a new everything. And maybe, just maybe, stop hurting.

"All right, so now I'm here," she said, brushing her bangs off her forehead, as if that action could brush the worry away from her mind, too. "You want to show me around this town you've raved so much about?"

Truth be told, Colton had done far more raving about Rachel Morris, the girl he was engaged to. He was clearly head over heels for the wedding planner he'd met a few months ago. He'd taken a job at the local fire department, and from what Katie could tell from his texts and phone calls, settled right into Stone Gap like he was born here. She shouldn't have been surprised—

Colton was the kind of guy who fit in anywhere, even with the half brothers he'd recently met. Katie, on the other hand, had never had the same kind of ease around people. Maybe it was from doing such a left-brained job, or maybe it was just that Colton had enough charm for the two of them combined.

"I can't leave now, sis, sorry. I just started my shift and I'm on the clock for a full twenty-four," he said. "But why don't you head over to the Stone Gap Inn, and I'll meet you there tomorrow night at suppertime? Tell Della I sent you. I stayed there until I rented a house in town. It's awesome. If anyone knows how to be a hostess, it's Della. She's my dad's wife, and I guarantee she's going to make you feel like a long lost member of the family."

Katie wasn't so sure about that. Right now, all she wanted was a room to herself and some time to think. "Sounds like a plan. Say…six o'clock?"

"On the dot." Then he winked. "More or less. You know you have to give me a ten-minute window, in either direction."

She rolled your eyes at him. "I swear, you do that on purpose."

Colton draped an arm over her shoulders and started walking her back to her car. "You are just a tiny bit too uptight, Piglet. Learn to loosen up. Run late once in a while. Get messy. Your life will be ten times more fun that way."

"And your life would be ten times easier if you just got a little more organized and on time."

Colton chuckled. "See you tomorrow, sis."

Katie climbed into her car and started the engine. She waved goodbye to her brother, then drove two miles away from downtown Stone Gap before turning on a pretty side street lined with trees. She'd been in town only for an hour and already knew her way around—such a difference from the crazy congestion of Atlanta. Okay, so she'd also studied a Google map of the town before making the drive from Atlanta, and written down the directions to the B and B after Colton had referred her to it when she'd broached the idea of visiting. But overall, Stone Gap was easy—easy to drive through, easy to enjoy.

This was what she wanted and needed, she told herself. A quiet, picturesque seaside town where she could...forget. Move on. *Take some time to process this*, the doctor had told her. *Don't expect to bounce right back into your normal life. You've had a loss, and you need time to deal with it.*

But how did one "process" a miscarriage? Katie's hand strayed to her belly, as if touching the place where the baby had been would change anything. Everything about her life was different now, had been for two months. Two months where she had buried her feelings and told herself she was okay. Then had a major meltdown at work, and lost the firm's two biggest clients. All in one day. The next day, her boss had sat her down and told her maybe it would be best for all involved if she moved on, a pretty little euphemism for being fired. Except Katie wasn't sure what to do next. How to move forward or move on.

For one brief moment—a handful of weeks, really—Katie had dared to consider a different life from the one she'd been living. She'd dreamed of detouring from the careful career path she'd been on. Quitting her job, because working eighty hours a week didn't jibe with being a mom, and maybe going out on her own or working at a smaller firm. She'd flipped through baby mag-

azines and surfed nursery design websites. She'd even
set up a Pinterest account, thinking she'd want a way to
organize and save all the things she had found.

And then one morning she'd woken up in pain, her
stomach curling in against her like a fist, and she'd
known, in that innate way a woman reads the whispers
of her body. Later that day, the doctor had confirmed
the wrenching truth Katie already knew.

The baby, the different life, the dream, were all gone.
She laid a hand on her stomach and could almost hear
it echoing inside. Katie had wanted to roll into a ball
in that hospital bed and cry, but instead, she'd gotten
dressed, checked out and gone to work.

Because she thought that would help her forget.

It hadn't.

And now, here she was, in a town not much bigger
than a postage stamp, looking for...peace. A direction.
She'd start, she decided, small. At the Stone Gap Inn.

She pulled into the driveway of the address Colton
had given her and looked up at the two-story white
antebellum-style house before her. A long, columned
front porch greeted visitors like a smile, anchored by
a swing on one end and two comfy rocking chairs on
the other. A rainbow of flowers flanked the walkway,
leading a happy march up to a bright red front door.
Katie half expected a girl in a corset and hoopskirt to
step onto the porch and offer visitors some sweet tea.

Just as she rang the bell, the front door opened and
a curvy red-haired woman in a floral apron greeted her
with a wide smile. "Why, hello! You must be Colton's
sister. He called me and told me you were on your way.
I'm Della." She put out her hand and shook with Katie.
"Della Barlow. I own this bed-and-breakfast, and run
it with my best friend, Mavis."

It was a fast, breathless, friendly introduction that rushed over Katie like a wave. "Uh, hi. Yes, I'm Colton's younger sister and he said he made a reservation for me?"

"He did indeed. Come right in." Della waved her in, and waited a beat while Katie stood in the foyer, mouth agape, and took in the grand staircase that zippered up the middle of the house.

It was like walking into the pages of *Gone with the Wind*. The staircase curved in at the center, with white risers marrying the wood treads and a carved railing that formed a graceful swoop up to the second floor. On the main floor, a formal parlor sat to the left, with a pair of vanilla love seats sitting on either side of an upright piano. Long, satiny cream drapes framed the floor-to-ceiling windows and a small rolltop desk against the far wall. The dining room was on the right, dominated by a long mahogany table with a wide spray of bright pink and white flowers at its center. The coffered ceiling provided the perfect backdrop to an elaborate chandelier filled with teardrop crystals. Shades of whites, creams and soft pastels filled every room, as inviting as sinking into a cloud. Katie loved it immediately.

"Welcome to the Stone Gap Inn," Della said, as she walked up the stairs with Katie right behind. "We just opened a few months ago, so we might still have a hiccup or two. The house was abandoned for years before Mavis and I bought it. It still had strong bones, though, being pre–Civil War, one of the few that survived those years. My husband and sons helped renovate it, along with some help from my wonderful soon-to-be daughter-in-law, who restores old houses. They all worked on it, top to bottom, but we kept as many period details as we could. Don't worry, though, we made sure all the plumbing and electricity is modern, along with Wi-Fi and satellite TV in each of the rooms."

Katie laughed. "It sounds perfect. In fact, it looks perfect. The house is stunning."

"Thank you. We love it, and so far, our guests have, too. They've all been so grateful to have a place to stay, ever since the original hotel in town closed up. The owner retired, moved to Minnesota to be near his grandkids, but was gracious enough to send all his customers to us. He said a B and B fits Stone Gap better, and I might be biased, but I happen to agree."

"I do, too," Katie said. "This place seems perfect for a small seaside town."

"Thank you. Mavis and I were looking for something to keep us busy in our golden years, and the way business has been going, we got our wish." Della laughed. "Anyway, I put you in the Charlotte Room," she said, opening a door as she spoke. "I hope you like it."

If Katie could have dreamed up a perfect bedroom, this would have been it. Pale green, bright white and accents of butter yellow made the room feel like a garden. A canopy bed dominated the space, looking more like a cloud than a place to sleep. Piles of pillows cascaded down the center of a thick white comforter. A low bench sat at the foot of the bed, with a basket filled with fluffy towels and soaps and bath salts on one end, a tray with mini bottles of water and a bowl of fresh fruit on the other. A ceiling-high armoire sat between the windows, and a thick white terry-cloth robe hung inside, just begging someone to slip it on, curl up in the armchair in the corner and read one of the books piled in the small bookcase.

Katie gasped. "Wow. It's gorgeous."

"I'm so glad you like the room. I'll give you some

time to get settled. If you want to join me in the kitchen for some coffee and fresh-baked cookies, come on downstairs." Della placed a room key in Katie's palm. "Welcome to Stone Gap."

Katie sank onto the bed after Della was gone, and thought yes, this was exactly what she needed. Maybe, just maybe, here in this town that seemed to wrap around her like a warm blanket, she could find a way to move forward again.

The scent of chocolate chip cookies drew Katie out of her nap and back downstairs an hour later. She'd slept better in that hour than she had in the last two months. It had to be the bed, or the total quiet that surrounded her, so unlike the constant hum of Atlanta.

In the kitchen, Della was at the stove, stirring something that smelled amazing. She turned when Katie entered the kitchen. "Coffee?"

"Do you have decaf?"

"I do indeed. Have a seat and—"

Katie waved off Della's instructions. She felt useless just relaxing like this. "Please, let me help."

"I'll do no such thing. Bed-and-breakfast means you get a place to sleep and breakfast served to you. But an inn means you get all that and more." Della grabbed a coffee mug and filled it with steaming brew. She placed it before Katie, along with cream and sugar in cute little cow-shaped containers. "Now, sit down and enjoy yourself. This is your vacation, dear."

"Will you please sit with me?" Katie said. For some reason, she didn't want to be alone. Maybe because when she was alone she tended to think, and that just brought everything back to the surface again. "Please."

Della glanced at the stove, then at the small table's

empty chair. "I think I will. My feet are barking at me to take a few minutes to sit on my duff. Besides, that crab chowder is done enough to cook all by itself." Della slipped out of the apron and hung it over the back of a chair, then poured herself a cup of coffee and added a splash of cream. "So, tell me, what brings you to Stone Gap?"

"Like you said, vacation. And..." Katie toyed with the mug. There was something friendly and open about Della Barlow that warmed the air between them and made Katie want to confide, a little, about all that was going on in her life. "And maybe find a job. I'm sort of between things and not sure where I want to go next. Colton raves about this town, and I thought I'd give it a couple weeks to see if it grows on me, too."

"If you're not careful, this town will wrap around your heart like ivy on an oak tree, pretty and strong. That's what it did to me, more than thirty-five years ago, when I moved here with my Bobby. 'Course, it helped that the man himself was also wrapped around my heart." Della smiled, clearly proud of her town and the man she'd married.

A man who had had an affair more than thirty years ago with Katie's mother, an affair that had produced Colton. Katie had seen pictures of her mother from those years, before her drinking took its toll. Vanessa Williams had been beautiful, with long dark hair, deep green eyes and a wide smile. In the years since Colton and Katie had been born, she'd morphed into a sullen, resentful woman who considered both her children as unwanted burdens.

But Della Barlow—she was obviously the kind of mother everyone wished they could have. It was clear she loved her sons and her husband, despite the brief bump their marriage had hit more than three decades ago. Katie had no doubt staying here would be like coming home.

"So, Katie, what do you do?" Della asked. "Or, a better question, what do you *want* to do, since not all of us work at our first-love jobs when we're young."

It had been a long time since Katie had thought about her ideal career. She felt like she was in middle school again, lying on her bed and looking up at the cracks in the ceiling. When she was eleven, she'd imagined they were paths, creeping like a spider out in different directions. If she took this path, she'd end up there, by that missing chunk of plaster. That path, and she'd connect with that path and that one, and end up fading into the window frame. The world had seemed open and endless back then, filled with crazy ideas like becoming a veterinarian and an actress and a chef, all at the same time. "I... I don't know. I've been an accountant for so long, I don't know anything else."

"Was that your dream, working with numbers?"

Katie scoffed. "No. I sort of fell into it. I was good at math, and I got a scholarship to college, as long as I enrolled in the accounting program. I've been doing this job so long, I don't know if I can do anything else."

Della waved that off. "Honey, you are as young as a baby bird. You still have time to go after whatever dream you want. Heck, I'm in my fifties and just now embarking on my dream." She gestured at the sunny yellow kitchen, the off-white cabinets, the wide plank floors. "Dare to do something different, while you aren't tied down to a family and a dog."

*Dare to do something different.* That was part of why Katie was here, because she didn't know what else to do with herself, except for something different. She couldn't stay one more second in Atlanta, where everything she looked at reminded her of what she had lost. "I don't even know where to start."

Della's hand covered hers. "Start with cookies."

"Cookies?"

"Of course. Everything's better with cookies." Della grinned. "And then, if you're interested in something temporary, I know someone who needs some help for the next few weeks. It's not a glamorous job, but I guarantee it'll be fun and not at all like accounting."

Katie took a bite out of a chewy chocolate chip cookie that melted against her tongue. Like the rest of the house and the owner herself, the cookies were the best ever. "What kind of job are you talking about?"

"Well…" Della took a sip of coffee, then wrapped her hands around the mug, "Sam Millwright is in need of a tutor. If you ask me, he needs a good nanny, too. I've met Charity Jacobs, the one working for him now, and she's a dear girl, but in over her head."

A tutor maybe, but a nanny? As in someone who watched kids all day? Katie had zero experience with children, unless one counted the couple summers she'd spent as a camp counselor. But that had been a team experience—never one where she was on her own, in charge of everything from sunup to sundown for a kid. She'd never had a younger sibling, never really babysat (okay, so she had watched her neighbor's Pomeranians twice, and commandeered her cousins almost every holiday meal, but that wasn't the same thing), never even watched a friend's child, let alone helped anyone with homework. And the thought of being with a baby…

"Sam's kids are just the cutest little things you ever did see. Libby just turned eight, and Henry is three," Della said. "You'd love them."

Three and eight. So not babies. Maybe doable. Maybe. But still, a nanny? Della was right, that was about as far removed from accountant as Katie could get. Except she had no desire to be a nanny, and not enough experience to even consider the job.

"Wait…did you say he needed a tutor, too?"

Della nodded. "Libby's struggling in school. Ever since her mom passed away, she's been having a hard time keeping up, poor thing. Sam's doing the best he can, but it's tough, being breadwinner and everything else at the same time. His regular babysitter up and quit a month ago, and Sam's been struggling ever since to find someone to watch the kids. He's got Charity filling in part of the time, but she's…" Della made a little face. "Anyway, I had the kids over here yesterday, trying to take the load off Sam, but you know, it's hard to run a business and watch two kids." She smiled. "Even if they're truly the nicest kids ever."

Couple of nice, sweet kids. How hard could it be? Katie would have to tutor only one of them, it seemed. And the extra money would be a godsend while she was debating her next move. Not to mention, as Della had said, it wasn't accounting. It wouldn't be a job that would require her to remember a million details or figure out complicated tax structures. It would be almost as easy as just staying home all day, except she'd hopefully be too busy to think. If the girl was eight, it wasn't like Katie was going to need a master's in English to tutor her. What was that, third grade? She could handle third grade homework help. And surely the math would be a breeze for her. As much as Katie said she wanted time to think, to breathe, just the thought of all that time in her head…

She'd rather be working. Doing something that

wasn't difficult, but still kept her mind from spinning. "Sure. I'll talk to him."

"Lovely!" Della grinned. "I'll give him a call quicker than a bunny running through a pepper patch."

Della did as she'd promised, calling up Sam Millwright a second later. Katie caught only half the conversation, but it was full of "you're going to love her" and "she's delightful" endorsements of Katie. Della dropped Colton's name into the conversation and that seemed to be the clincher. Della hung up the phone, then scribbled an address on a piece of paper. "Here's his address," she said. "He said to be there at eight thirty tomorrow morning and he'll give you an interview."

"Sounds like a plan," Katie said, taking the paper. It wasn't moving on or moving forward, but it wasn't standing still, either, and for now, that was enough.

## Chapter Two

It was only a little after eight in the morning and already Sam had resorted to bribery. "If you eat your breakfast, Libby Bear, I'll let you have a cookie."

Probably not the healthiest bribe, but at this point, after dealing with the kids for two hours—thanks to Henry waking up at the crack of way-too-early—Sam was desperate. Hell, most days he was desperate. Between the kids and an overly eager one-year-old golden retriever, Sam felt outnumbered, outmaneuvered and out of ideas.

"Miss Della's cookies?" Libby asked with a wary look. "Because your cookies smell weird."

As in *eau de burned*. Della Barlow had taken one look at the snack Sam had packed for the kids yesterday and baked them three dozen chocolate chip pity cookies. Thank God, because Sam couldn't cook his way out of a paper bag. He wasn't much good at housework or doing ponytails or answering tough questions from a still-grieving three- and eight-year-old. What he was good at was corporate real estate. Or at least he had been, until the agency he worked for went belly-up. All the profits on million-dollar deals he'd brought into the agency had been frittered away by the owner, leaving the coffers dry when it came to making the payments on their own building. Sam had walked into work last Monday and found a for-sale sign on the door, and the locks changed, most likely by the bank. All his pending deals went up in smoke as panicked clients ran off to other agents, and the commission check Sam had been counting on to pay the bills had bounced higher than a new tennis ball.

It was partly his own fault. All the signs of a business in trouble had been there, but he'd been too distracted, trying to run a household and keep the kids fed and clothed and going to bed on time, to pay attention. He'd done the one thing he couldn't afford to do—turned his focus away from his job—and it had nearly cost him everything.

He had an interview with the agency's biggest competitor later this morning. The problem? He had yet to find regular child care. One would think it wouldn't be hard, but the three nannies he had met so far had been like the Three Stooges: incompetent, irresponsible and insane. He'd hired Charity Jacobs a couple weeks ago. She was okay, but not exactly Nanny of the Year, nor was she interested in taking on the job full-time. She kept saying something about needing to see her boyfriend. Half the time, Charity looked terrified to be left alone with the kids. But so far she'd kept them fed and clean, and that was more than the others had done.

On top of that, there was Libby and the constant

worry about her falling behind. Third grade was a pivotal year for math skills, her teacher had said, with the kind of impending doom in her voice that suggested Libby would end up a panhandler if she didn't grasp the basics this year. She needed a tutor and Sam needed a miracle.

Thank God Della had called yesterday and promised the perfect candidate in Colton's little sister.

Sam liked Colton. Liked all the Barlows, in fact. He'd met Colton, half brother to Mac, Luke and Jack, at a town picnic a couple months ago. There'd been a rousing and surprisingly competitive game of cornhole, which Colton was close to winning until Sam made his final shot. The two men had laughed, then shared a couple beers and found a common ground in fishing, something Colton had done a lot of recently with his future father-in-law and his fiancée. Sam and he had hung out a few times since, now that Colton had moved to Stone Gap on a permanent basis.

Libby hopped down off the chair and started twirling. Her skirt swung out around her in a rising bell. "I want ballet lessons. Can I have ballet lessons?"

Ballet lessons. Another thing he'd have to schedule and run to. Libby made a constant argument in favor of the lessons by wearing an old, tattered ballerina dress, a Halloween costume from years ago, pretty much every day. He'd wanted Libby to wear jeans and a T-shirt to school today. Libby had thrown a fit, pitching herself onto the floor and sobbing, saying that Mommy had bought her the ballerina dress and she really wanted to wear it—

And Sam caved. He'd also caved on letting the kids watch cartoons while they ate, though Bugs Bunny and friends hadn't exactly inspired anyone to take a single bite yet.

He glanced at the still untouched waffle on Libby's plate. "Libby, you need to eat your breakfast so we can get to school and I can get Henry over to the community center." He had just enough time to give the tutor a quick interview, drop the kids at school by nine and get to his interview at nine fifteen.

Libby let out a sigh that sounded way too grown-up. "We don't have school today."

"Of course you have school today. It's Tuesday."

Libby shook her head. "Miss McCarthy said we didn't. There's some big meeting for the teachers or something."

Sam crossed to the fridge, moving menus and notes and drawings around until he finally found the school calendar, tacked in place by a thick magnet. He ran his finger down to today's date—

No School. In-Service Teacher Day.

He started to curse, then stopped himself. Now what was he supposed to do? He pulled out his phone and texted Charity. No school today. Need you ASAP.

"And Uncle Ty said the community center is closed today. 'Cuz he had to fix the bathroom or something."

"There's no storytime today?" What else could go wrong this morning?

Libby shrugged. "Can I go play?"

"Eat your breakfast first." *While I come up with a miracle.* He had forty-five minutes until his interview. Forty-five minutes to get Charity over here and interview this new girl for the tutor job.

Libby shook her head. "I don't like those waffles. I like the ones…"

Her voice trailed off, but Sam could fill in the blank

himself. She liked the ones her mommy had made, before Mommy had been killed by a drunk driver. The year and a half since then had passed in a blur, with Sam juggling a job and the kids and babysitters and his grief. He'd thought he was doing a good job, until he lost first Mrs. Rey, the best nanny in the world, who had moved to Florida to be with her grandkids, then a few weeks later, his job. He'd tried to step in and do it all, but he wasn't much good at being two parents in one. Time, he told himself, time fixed everything.

Except when he was running late. "Libby, you need to eat because I need to—"

She stopped spinning and crossed her arms over her chest. "No."

Lately, Libby had mastered defiance. She wasn't outright disobedient, just enough to add another stress to Sam's day.

From his booster seat at the other end of the kitchen table, Henry let out a shriek of support. Sam turned to his son. "Hey, buddy, want to eat breakfast?"

Henry shook his head.

"Do you want something else? Just say it, buddy, and I'll get you whatever you want."

Henry stared at his father for one long moment. Sam waited, his heart in his throat. Maybe this time…

Instead, Henry picked up his waffle and flung it on the floor. Before Sam could react, the golden retriever dashed in and stole a bonus meal.

That made Libby laugh, while she tossed her waffle at the dog, too. "Get it, Bandit. Get it!"

"Libby—"

But she was already gone, tearing off to the living room to snatch up the TV remote and raise the volume to deafening levels. Henry saw his own opportunity for escape, and clambered down from the chair and over to the giant box of Legos that Sam had forgotten to put up on the top shelf. Before Sam could say "don't touch that," Henry had knocked it onto the floor, releasing a cavalcade of miniature bricks.

And then the doorbell rang.

The dog started barking. Libby started peppering her father with questions about who was there, was it Miss Della, was it the mailman, was it Barney the dinosaur. Sam closed his eyes for a too-brief second, then strode down the hall and pulled open the door.

One of the most beautiful women Sam had ever seen stared back at him, with big brown doe-like eyes peeking out from under long dark wavy hair. She wore a pencil skirt that hugged her curves, a satiny pink blouse and dark pumps that raised her from what he guessed was a normal height of about five foot three. "Uh, I'm Katie Williams," she said, while he continued to stare. "I'm here to interview for the tutor position? I'm sorry I'm a few minutes early."

The tutor. Of course. Already, he'd forgotten about her appointment. Maybe he was the one who should have eaten his breakfast. Or, for that matter, had a cup of coffee. Thus far, Sam was lucky he'd had enough time to throw on some clothes and brush his teeth. And given that Charity hadn't responded to his text yet, that meant he still didn't have anyone to watch Libby, and his interview was in less than forty-five minutes… "Oh, yes, I'm sorry. I—" He threw up his hands and gave up trying to formulate any kind of excuse. How did he encapsulate months of feeling overwhelmed into one sentence? "It's been a morning and a half. Katie Williams—Colton's little sister, right?"

"Yes."

Which made her probably only a couple years younger than Sam. He didn't know why that mattered so much, but it suddenly did. "Colton's a great guy."

"Who's here?" Libby skidded to a stop beside him and poked her head around the door. "Hi. I'm Libby."

Katie bent down. "Hi, Libby. I'm Katie." She raised her gaze and peered at the space behind Sam. "And who's that?"

Libby turned. "Oh, that's my little brother, Henry. He's shy."

Katie wiggled her fingers in Henry's direction. "Hi, Henry. I'm Katie."

Henry stood at the corner for a second longer, then dashed back into the living room. He never uttered a peep. Not that Sam had expected him to. Henry had almost completely stopped talking after his mother died. Sam had taken his son to doctor after doctor, spent hours searching the internet, but the conclusion was the same—Henry would talk when he was ready.

Lord, how Sam missed the sound of Henry's voice. The curiosity in the lilting questions he used to ask. Sam's heart ached, literally ached, for the things he had lost. The things he couldn't change.

Libby, the more outgoing of the two kids, just kept looking up at Katie with obvious curiosity. "Do you like dogs?" Libby asked.

Katie smiled. "I love dogs."

One point in favor of Katie Williams. Hopefully, she liked dogs with plenty of puppy energy, because he could feel Bandit nudging past him. Just as Sam reached for the dog's collar, Bandit leaped, paws landing on Katie's chest. She stumbled back, and for a long, heart-stopping second, Sam thought she was going to fall down his porch stairs. Visions of hospitals and lawsuits popped into his mind. He reached for her, caught her hand, just as she recovered her balance and swayed forward. But then she overcorrected, and swayed straight into his chest.

"Oh, God. I'm… I'm sorry," she said, jerking away from him.

He knew he should say the same, but for one long second there he hadn't been sorry at all that she had touched him. Maybe it was because he'd been alone for so long, or maybe it was because she was one of the most beautiful women he'd ever seen, but either way, a little frisson of electricity had run through Sam when Katie touched his chest. It was chased by a wave of guilt. Wendy had been dead for only a year and a half. What was he doing, reacting to another woman like that?

"I'm the one who needs to apologize. My, uh, dog is still learning his manners," Sam said, and thought it would be a good thing if his owner remembered his. "But please come in, have a seat while we talk. I can lock Bandit up if you want."

"Oh, no, the dog is fine. I love dogs, remember? Really." Katie started to follow Sam into the house, with Bandit hot on her heels.

"You can come with me," Libby said. She put her hand in Katie's and tugged her down the hall. "My father says I gotta be nice to people who come over to the house."

*My father. Not Daddy.* He hadn't heard Daddy, or even Dad in a long time. He bit back another sigh.

"And he's supposed to be nice, too," Libby added, giving Sam a pointed glare.

Katie looked up at Sam and smiled. She had a nice smile. A really nice smile. "Is that so?"

"Yup. 'Cuz sometimes he's grumpy," Libby added, thumbing in the direction of Sam.

Sam groaned. That was the problem with kids. They said too much and always at the wrong time. "I'm not grumpy. Just...stressed."

"How come?" Libby asked.

He ruffled his daughter's hair. She stiffened, an almost imperceptible amount, but the distance was there. The easy relationship he'd had with his eldest had also disappeared in the last year and a half. Sam put on a bright face, pretending, as he always did, that he didn't notice. That they were all just fine. "Because *some people* feed their breakfast to the dog."

Katie bit back a laugh. "My brother used to do that."

"Not you?"

"Of course not. I was the good one." Katie smiled when she said that, which sent his mind spiraling down a couple paths that were not appropriate for interviewing the tutor. Yeah, he definitely had been alone too long. That was all it was.

Sam cleared his throat and gestured toward the dining room table. The kitchen was a mess—as was typical pretty much every day of the week—with dirty dishes piled in the sink, breakfast crumbs scattered across the table and countertops, and a set of muddy paw prints running circles around the table. They never used the dining room, which meant it was relatively clean, if he ignored the light coating of dust on everything. "Libby, go watch cartoons with Henry."

"But I wanna—"

"Go watch cartoons with Henry. Please." He prayed Libby wouldn't argue, that she would just do what he said.

Libby stood her ground a moment longer, but then

the sounds of Bugs Bunny and Daffy Duck drew her into the other room. Sam had a brief moment of peace in his house, which meant he'd better get this interview done fast, before Katie realized things here were actually more like a zoo, and she ran out the door, like more than one nanny he'd interviewed.

"Is there any chance you also want to be a nanny?" he asked, only half joking. Still no text back from Charity.

"I've never been a nanny, or a tutor," she said. "I'm a CPA, but I'm…looking for a new direction for now. I'm in town for a couple weeks while I think about my career options."

A CPA? What had Della been thinking? Talk about overqualified for the job.

"Do you have *any* experience with kids?" He should have realized that when she showed up on his doorstep. Any tutor in her right mind wouldn't be wearing heels and a figure-hugging pencil skirt.

He glanced at his phone again. Nothing from Charity. Damn. The last thing he wanted to do was take the kids with him. He'd had to do that a few times with client appointments and the results had been…disastrous to say the least. He was still paying for the marker decorations that Henry had drawn on a custom-made leather sofa in one client's office. It was almost impossible to carry on a conversation of any kind of substance with the kids in the room. And for him to show up at an interview with them…

He might as well kiss the job goodbye. "You know, maybe we should reschedule. This is a crazy busy morning for me. If you could come back—"

"No!" Libby's shriek cut through the air like a knife. "No!"

Sam bolted out of the chair and charged down the hall, his heart a tight ball in his throat. He never should have left the kids alone in the living room. This was how awful things happened, and if there was one thing that would break Sam, it would be one of his kids getting hurt. Or worse. *Please be okay, please be okay.*

It was probably only ten yards from the dining room to the living room, but to Sam, it felt like ten thousand. "Libby? You okay?"

"Henry took my bear when I was playing with it! He's hurting him! Tell him to stop!"

It took Sam a second to process the fact that Libby and Henry were both fine. Just engaged in a tug-of-war over a stuffed bear. Libby's voice was at decibels usually reserved for rock concerts, the sound nearly outpaced by Henry's screams. No words, just the frustrated screams that Sam had heard too much of in the last year and a half.

"Henry, give Libby back her bear."

But Henry didn't listen. Instead, he tugged harder, at the same time that Libby tugged in the opposite direction. There was a horrible tearing sound, and then an explosion of fiberfill in the air. The kids tumbled onto the carpet, each holding half a bear, like some kind of biblical division of property.

The sobs multiplied in volume. Libby was screaming at Henry and Henry was screaming back, and Sam just wanted to quit. Quit being a terrible father. Quit being the chief everything when he didn't know what the hell he was doing. Just run away somewhere that was quiet and peaceful and clean.

His wife would have known what to do. Wendy had had a way with the kids, a calming presence that seemed to bring everyone back to earth in seconds. God, he missed her, and how she could handle all these things that he sucked at. Wendy would have known whose bear that was, but Sam—Sam couldn't even remember buying the bear.

"No!" Libby screamed again. "Look what you did, Henry! You ruined him!"

While Sam stood there, at a loss, with two kids in the throes of tantrums, Bandit ran into the fray and grabbed a chunk of bear, then darted into the corner like he'd scored a new chew toy. And Libby started to sob.

Great, just great. Now how was he supposed to fix this?

He stayed immobile, frozen with indecision, afraid of doing the wrong thing, making it worse. Katie brushed past him. "Don't cry, Libby. I can sew this," she said, bending down in the space between the kids. "Fix him up as good as new."

Libby swiped at her nose with the back of her arm. "You can?"

Katie nodded while she gathered up the fiberfill and began stuffing it into the bear's belly. Henry quieted, too, and just watched, eyes wide. "I learned how to sew when I was your age. If you want, I can teach you how."

"*He* doesn't know how to sew," Libby said, jabbing another thumb in her father's direction.

Katie shot Sam a grin. "Some daddies don't and some mommies don't. But if I teach you, then you'll know and next time you can fix—" she tapped the bear's decapitated head, then turned to Henry "—what's his name?"

Henry just stared at her. His fist clenched around the puff of stuffing.

"A bear's gotta have a name." Katie smiled at Henry, then inched closer. Sam started to go in there, to stop her, to tell her Henry was just going to run from her, but Katie kept talking, her voice calm and soft. Mesmerizing. "When I was a little girl, I had a bear like this one. I used to get scared a lot when it was dark, and my big brother, Colton, would find my bear and bring it to me. He would tuck me in and tell me stories until I stopped being scared and I fell asleep. I shared my bear with my brother sometimes, too, and Colton even gave Willard his own nicknames. My bear was my bestest friend when I was little, and I bet this guy is your friend, huh?"

Henry nodded.

"My bear's name was Willard, but my brother nicknamed him Patch, because he was fixed so many times he had a patch over his belly. He wasn't near as nice as your bear. So," Katie said, giving the bodyless bear a little tap on the nose, "what's his name? I gotta know his name so I can fix him, and tell him it's all going to be okay."

Henry shifted from foot to foot. Even though Libby knew the answer, she stood silently behind Katie, staring, waiting, just like Sam was. Katie just gave Henry a patient smile.

Then, very slowly, Henry held out his hand and uncurled his tight fist. A pouf of fiberfill sprang up like a daisy in his palm. "Henry help fix George?"

Henry's little voice rang like a bell in the quiet of the living room. Libby turned to her father, mouth agape. Sam put a hand on his chest, sure he was hearing things.

Henry had *spoken*. A handful of words, but to Sam, it might as well have been the Gettysburg Address. *Henry had spoken*—and Sam's heart was so full, he was sure it would burst just like the bear.

Katie nodded. "Of course Henry can help. And for the record, I think George is a terrific name for a bear."

"T'ank you," Henry said quietly, then he dropped the puff of stuffing into Katie's lap.

Sam swallowed the lump in his throat. He didn't give a damn that Katie Williams had come in here looking like she was walking into court. He didn't give a damn that she didn't have much, if any, experience. If she could get through to Henry, he had little doubt that she could get through to Libby, too, and restore his daughter's love for school. Katie had brought about a miracle that no one else had. She'd shifted the tides in a family too long on a rolling ocean, and for Sam, that was résumé enough. "You're hired."

# Chapter Three

Katie wasn't so sure she'd heard Sam right. She was hired? Just like that?

And did she even really want the job?

She'd be with these two kids for at least an hour at a time if she became Libby's tutor. Small children with winsome faces and those little-kid voices. The very thing she had been looking forward to, before—

Could she do it? Or would it be too painful?

Katie was still kneeling on the floor between Henry and Libby, holding the tattered remains of George the teddy bear. Libby, who seemed ten times older than her age, came over and stood in front of her. She propped her fists on her tiny hips and cocked her brown curls to one side. "Are you gonna stay?" Libby's eyes, so like her father's, clouded. "Just 'cuz, you know, 'cuz our mommy died and...and... I really wanna fix George."

The naked honesty and pain in Libby's face was al

most too much to bear. Katie could see the yearning for a mother, the way that loss had impacted the little girl in a thousand ways, in the empty shadows in Libby's eyes. Katie's heart broke for Libby, and for little Henry, standing there silently, his thumb in his mouth, just watching her. Katie had no doubt Sam loved his kids, but he was clearly overwhelmed, and these two little ones needed someone. Being a tutor wouldn't be all that tough, she figured, and she could help people who clearly needed help.

And given the way the two kids were staring at her, with a mix of hope and wary trust in their faces, she knew they wanted that someone to be her. It felt nice to be needed, even if only for this little while. Katie knew what it was like to crave a parent who engaged. Who cared. Katie wasn't going to be their parent, but maybe she could help fill some of the gaps.

"Okay," Katie said to Libby. "I'll stay. We can fix George, if you have some thread and a needle?"

Sam put out his hands. "If we do, I have no idea where."

"No problem. I'll pick some up this week." She bent down to Henry's level again. "George is gonna need some special thread to be fixed. Can you wait for me to bring that over?"

Henry gave her a reluctant nod.

Libby ran into the other room, then hurried back. She thrust a stuffed dog into Henry's arms. "Here. You can play with Puppy until then. But don't break him."

Henry grinned, then clutched the stuffed animal close to his chest.

"That was very nice, Libby," Katie said.

"Thanks." A slow smile spread across Libby's face, then she turned and grabbed Henry's hand. "Come on, Henry. Let's watch *SpongeBob*." The two of them plopped on the sofa, with Libby working the remote to switch to the underwater cartoon.

Katie rose and turned toward Sam. She'd accepted a job she wasn't sure she wanted, without knowing a single thing about the hours, the pay, anything. That was as far outside the realm of how she normally operated as she could get. "So, maybe we should discuss the details."

He grinned. She liked his smile. It was warm, friendly, like the way brownies made you feel when you first pulled them out of the oven. He was a handsome man, six foot two, trim and muscular, with close-cropped medium brown hair and dark brown eyes. He was wearing a T-shirt that seemed molded to his chest—not that she was complaining—and a pair of jeans that hung low on his hips. His feet were bare, and there was just something about the intimacy of that that made Katie feel like she was intruding in his space. From the moment she'd seen him, standing at the door, annoyed and flustered, she'd felt this warmth in her gut that rippled through her veins.

His phone buzzed and he glanced down. "My appointment was just moved to nine thirty, which means I have time to finally have a cup of coffee. Do you want one?"

"Coffee would be great." And maybe with a mug in her hands she'd stop staring at the hot widower's body. She followed him out to the kitchen, which looked pretty much like the tornado from *The Wizard of Oz* had just blown through. Dirty dishes teetered in the sink, a stack of newspapers lay scattered across the counter, crumbs littered the floor and the space around the toaster, and there was a pile of dirty laundry bulging out from the laundry room door like an impending avalanche.

Yup, Sam was clearly stressed. A lot stressed.

"Uh, sorry, I think I have a second clean cup here." He opened a cabinet door, another, then finally unearthed two mugs from the back of the third cabinet he looked in. Sam poured her a cup of coffee, then held it out. "I don't have any cream, but I do have milk and sugar."

"Black is fine. Thank you." She sipped the coffee, a surprisingly rich and good brew, and kept her back to the counter rather than taking the only free chair at the kitchen table. The others had stacks of mail and toys piled on them, as if the rest of the house was coming for lunch.

"Uh, sorry." Sam rushed forward and scooped a pile of things off one of the chairs. He started to put it on the table, then thought better of that and pivoted to the left, depositing the toys and books onto the floor by a drooping and browning potted plant. "It's, uh, been hard to work and watch the kids and…well, my last nanny quit a few weeks ago and the new one isn't as good as the other one, and…" He let out a breath. "Mostly, I'm just not good at this juggling thing."

She laughed. "It's fine, really. And made all that much better by a man who admits he can't do it all."

"I definitely can't do it all." Sam gestured toward the empty seat and waited for her to take it before he sat opposite her. "At work, I can juggle multiple clients and deals, but here, I'm bested regularly by a three-year-old and a third-grader."

"You seem to be doing fine." Okay, so maybe she was generously stretching the definition of the word *fine*.

He ran a hand through his hair, a move that made him seem more vulnerable somehow. "I'm not, but thanks for saying that. I really need some help, at least until Libby gets caught up. It's a short-term job, if that's okay. Feel free to say no. You are incredibly overqualified to teach math to a third-grader."

She didn't want to get into the reasons why an over-qualified CPA would take on a tutoring job. "That works for me. I wasn't really looking for anything permanent, so I'm flexible with whatever schedule you want." It shouldn't be too hard, right? Though the thirtyish man across from her didn't seem to have it under control, so why would she think she could do it better?

"Aren't you here on vacation?" Sam asked. "I'd hate to take up whatever free time you have. You said two weeks, which, if you can work with Libby regularly, should give her a good head start on getting caught up. I'll worry about a more permanent solution once I find one." He sighed. "Anyway, I really don't want to monopolize your time off."

"It's only sort of a vacation." How did she begin to explain the meltdown in the office, the clear signs that she needed to get away, to leave town, to start over? How once she'd arrived here and had more than five minutes of quiet, all those thoughts and memories and emotions she'd been avoiding washed over her like a tidal wave? And how the one thing she was banking on with being Sam's tutor was that it would leave her too busy to think? "This job works perfectly with my plans."

"Well, I am glad to hear that." Relief washed over her at his words. He mentioned a decent hourly rate,

and she agreed. His phone buzzed and he pulled it out
of his pocket, then read the text on the screen. "Thank
God. Charity is on her way over. Normally, I bring
Henry to storytime at the community center my uncle
runs, and Charity picks him up from there. But since
Libby doesn't have school today, it's easiest if I just
leave Henry here. She can watch him while you work
with Libby. If it's at all possible, do you think you could
start with Libby today?"

"Today?"

"If you can't, well, I understand, but Charity is still
new and though she's great, she gets overwhelmed when
she has both kids. With you here, that should help her
out. I'd take them, but I have this job interview and I
can't take the kids because I'm still paying for Henry's
'creativity'—" Sam rolled his eyes and made air quotes
"—at the last place I interviewed at."

She bit back a laugh. Sam was so clearly out of his
depth with these kids that she couldn't help but want
to make it easier on him. Plus, if she started today, she
wouldn't have a long, endless day stretching ahead of
her with nothing to fill the hours. Colton was sleeping,
after getting off his shift at the fire station, and wouldn't
be available until dinnertime. "Today sounds perfect."

"Great. Thank you." He glanced over at the sofa.
"The kids are quiet right now, so if it's okay, I'm going
to run upstairs, take a shower and get ready. Charity
should be here in ten minutes, but I have to leave in...
eleven. If you don't mind waiting, I'd appreciate it. Give
me five minutes. Ten, tops. Okay?"

"I think I can handle this for ten minutes." She gave
him a soft smile, and tried to pretend a part of her wasn't

thinking about the hunky man before her taking off his clothes and stepping into a shower.

When Sam went upstairs, Katie wandered into the living room. This space, too, looked like the aftermath of a tornado, complete with a second carpet of tiny little bricks. Now that it was just her and the two kids, she wasn't quite sure what to do or how to engage them. She glanced at the television. Some cartoon sponge-shaped guy was running around in his underwear and letting out an annoying nasal laugh. "Hey, guys, what are you watching?"

"*SpongeBob,*" Libby said. "He lives in the water. With Mr. Krabs. And Patrick."

"Sounds, uh…educational." Whatever happened to *Sesame Street*? *The Electric Company*? Shows she remembered and understood.

A commercial came on and Libby turned toward Katie. "Do you have a boyfriend?"

"Uh…no." She'd *had* a boyfriend. Who had dumped her the second he found out she was pregnant. She'd never in a million years thought nerdy Leonard Backstrom, another accountant at the firm, would be the one to break up first. He'd talked a lot about wanting to settle down, buying a house in an up-and-coming neighborhood, then starting joint retirement and 529 accounts. One stupid night when they both had too much to drink, and his tune had changed. He was, apparently, all talk and no real action. Last she heard, Leonard was dating Meredith the receptionist. He'd never even called Katie after she told him she was pregnant, as if he figured it was all her problem now.

After Katie had accepted that she was pregnant, she'd begun to think of a future with a child. A future of just the two of them. Those thoughts had grown into dreams, a plan—

Until she'd started cramping ten weeks later and lost everything.

So yeah, that was the complicated answer to *do you have a boyfriend?* Probably best to keep it to *uh...no.*

"My father says I can't have a boyfriend until I'm thirty," Libby said, and once again, Katie was struck by how mature she sounded. She sat down and Libby leaned closer. "Are you thirty?"

Katie laughed. "Almost. I'm twenty-nine."

"My father is thirty-four." Libby held up all her fingers, then flashed the digits three times. "That's old."

"You won't think so when you're thirty-four." Interacting with these kids wasn't so hard. She could do this. And she and Libby seemed to get along okay. The tutor thing should work out perfectly. In and out, an hour at a time. No biggie.

Libby considered that, then glanced over at Henry. "That's my brother. He's three."

Henry sat there, a blanket curled in one hand, just watching the exchange. He was a quiet kid. Probably easy to handle, Katie was sure. "He seems very nice."

Libby's nose wrinkled. "He smells funny and he takes my toys and he makes a mess with his food."

Katie laughed. "My brother was like that. But you know, he grew up to be really cool. Henry probably will, too."

Libby's nose wrinkled more. "My father makes me eat vegetables."

"Vegetables are good for you," Katie said.

"Are you gonna make me eat vegetables?"

"I don't think that's in my job description."

"Good. Because I don't wanna eat them," Libby said.

"Libby Bear, be nice to Katie. She's only here to help you with your schoolwork. No broccoli involved." Sam's voice came from behind Katie. She turned in her seat and her pulse did a little skip.

If she'd thought he looked handsome in a T-shirt and jeans, he was positively devastating in a suit and tie, with his hair still wet from the shower, smelling of fresh aftershave and soap. He was adjusting the cuffs on his white shirt, and for some reason, she thought that was one of the sexiest things she'd ever seen. Everything from the dark blue windowpane-pattern suit to the crimson tie at his neck and the black wingtip shoes gave him an air of power and manly confidence. Like a lion stepping onto the prairie and claiming his turf.

"I don't want to do schoolwork!" Libby sat back on the couch, crossed her arms over her chest and let out a huff. "You're mean."

"Yup. I am." He gave Katie a grin. "Still want the job?"

A job that came with perks like seeing Sam in a suit? Sign her up. "Yes, yes. I… I do."

Good Lord, she was stammering. The confident partner at the accounting firm had been replaced by a hormone-crazed teenage girl. She got to her feet, smoothed her skirt and cleared her throat. "Perhaps it's best if we went over any additional rules or expectations now."

He didn't say anything for a second, then he seemed to refocus, and nodded. "Yes. Yes, you're right."

She followed him out to the kitchen and they took the same seats as before. "So, do you have a list of things that Libby needs to work on?"

"Her teacher said she needed help with times tables and three-digit addition and subtraction problems. The whole carrying the one thing, you know? Then there are word problems, which I swear were created to stump parents." He laughed.

"Lucy has seven cantaloupes and Dave has three apples, so what time will the train arrive at the station?" Katie asked.

"Exactly." He crossed to a pile of papers on the back kitchen counter and riffled through it. "Her teacher sent home a list that I've got here somewhere. My late wife was the planner and organizer. Since she's been gone, I've just kind of...held on for dear life. I'm not very good at this whole juggling act."

"My childhood was like that. I guess it's why I'm the opposite. I like everything to add up, and for all the columns to balance."

He pulled a sheet out of the pile, then handed it to Katie as he sat down again. "Well, one thing I've learned about having kids, no matter how organized and planned you make your days, you're never going to get everything to add up perfectly. Kids..." His voice trailed off and his gaze drifted to the sofa, where Libby and Henry were laughing at the antics of the sponge and his starfish friend. "Kids change everything."

"Yes," she said softly, and her hand strayed to her empty belly, "yes, they do."

He turned back and his gaze met hers, and held, for one long second. "Thank you."

The praise made her shift in her seat. "I haven't even done my job yet. Why are you thanking me?"

"Because..." Sam's face clouded and his eyes filled, and his voice grew rough. "Because you got Henry to

talk. I haven't heard his voice in a long, long time."
Then, as if the emotion was too much, Sam got to his
feet and grabbed a piece of paper and a pen from the
middle of the table. He cleared his throat and dropped
his gaze to the paper. "I'm going to write down my cell
number. Call or text me if you have any problems. I'll
be back after the interview, and Charity will be here
any second, so you should be fine. Libby has a folder of
practice sheets in her backpack that her teacher needs
her to work on. If you and Libby get along, and this
works for you, we'll talk about a schedule for the next
week when I get home. Sound good?"

She rose, too, and closed the gap between them to
take the paper, adding it to the one from Libby's teacher.
"Sounds good."

His gaze dropped to her lips, then to her eyes.
"And...thank you."

She was close. Too close to him. But she couldn't
seem to make her feet move in reverse. "You...you said
that already."

"I'm sorry. I'm just...distracted."

She wanted to ask him if that was because of her or
the job interview or something else, but the doorbell
rang just then. The dog started barking, the kids started
shouting, and a second later, a sullen twenty-year-old
was in the kitchen, and the moment was gone. Charity
looked about as happy to be there as a grandparent at
a death metal concert.

Sam made the introductions and filled Charity in on
Katie's role. "Call me or text me if either of you have
any problems at all. I'll be back before you know it."

A few minutes later, Sam was gone. Charity leaned

against the counter, her arms crossed over her slim frame. "Good luck," she said.

"Thanks, but I'm sure I'll be fine. It's just third grade math and reading."

Charity scoffed. "Yup. And with Libby, that's about as much fun as negotiating a nuclear war. So I say again, good luck."

Charity stalked out of the room, scooped up Henry and took him into the backyard to play on the swing set. Katie turned and saw Libby standing in the doorway, arms crossed, defiance in her eyes.

*Good luck.*

## Chapter Four

"Welcome to the team, Sam." Hank Osborn got to his feet and put his hand out. "We look forward to working with you."

Relief filled Sam. He had a job again. Thank God. If there was one worry that had consumed his every thought, it was how he was going to provide for his family. There was no wife to fall back on for an additional income, no partner to help pick up the slack. It was all on Sam's shoulders, a weight that damned near seemed to kill him some days. The house, the kids, the bills, the…the loneliness. That was a place in his mind he didn't dare dwell upon. That hole in his world, that empty spot in his bedroom, his bathroom. The way he missed Wendy's chirpy *good mornings* and her sweet, whispered *good nights*.

Sam pushed those thoughts away. One thing at a time—right now, he had the job. That alone made him want to shout from the rooftops. Instead he settled for a professional smile and a nod of gratitude.

"When I looked back over some of your deals, I was really impressed," Hank went on. "You did a great job negotiating that multi-property deal in Raleigh. One of my guys was trying to win that battle, but you had that creative idea to find tenants before the negotiations started, and we were out of the running before the race even started. That was one hell of a deal, son."

"Thank you."

"And I expect the same kind of ingenious thinking while you're working for me. I like a man who thinks outside the box. Sound good?"

"Definitely, sir." Sam was glad to find Hank was a lot like him when it came to getting the deal done. It was part of the reason he had liked the gregarious older man immediately. Hank had owned Osborn Properties for thirty years, and brought it from a small one-man operation up to a three-office company with two dozen brokers, serving all of North Carolina and parts of the rest of the South. It was a big step for Sam, going from the small company he'd been at before to this one. The opportunities and support structure would be better, but the performance expectations were also going to be higher.

"I'll put you on the Midway Mall project right away," Hank said, handing Sam a file folder. "We have five open spaces in there, and want to get them filled before the mall opens in two months. One hundred percent capacity by opening day. Nothing less. Think you can do that?"

A huge task. It would mean working a lot of hours, and he still had a shaky child care solution. But the last thing he wanted to say to his new boss was no. "Yes, sir."

"One more thing," Hank said as he came around the desk. He put a hand on Sam's shoulder and walked with him to the door. "Don't call me sir. That's for my dad or my grandpa. Around here, I'm just Hank."

"Sounds good... Hank." Sam shook hands with the other man one more time, then said goodbye and headed out the door. It wasn't until he got in his car that he allowed himself a giant exhalation of relief.

The loss of his job had weighed on him like a ten-ton Mack truck. But now, with Hank's offer—even if it came wrapped up in some pretty high expectations—that weight had been lifted. He had a job, Libby had a tutor—a beautiful and capable tutor at that—and life was finally improving, a little at a time.

He wound his way through the bucolic, hilly roads of Stone Gap, mentally running through a list of potential clients to call for the mall project. If he could talk to Charity and convince her to sign on long-term for babysitting, then achieving Hank's goal was doable. Plus, if things had gone well with Katie today, then all the better—it would get Libby back on track in math and reading, and reduce the number of arguments he had with his daughter.

Not to mention how Katie had transformed his little family in the space of a morning. Sam could still hear the echoes of Henry's voice in his head. His son had turned a corner today, thanks to Katie Williams, and it was one that Sam hoped spelled good changes ahead.

Such a small thing, one that too many people took for granted, but oh, how he never would again. He owed Katie something huge — something impossible to grasp—for bringing his little boy back from the world of silence. Even if it was only a tiny step forward, and lasted only a moment, Sam would be eternally grateful.

For the first time in a long time, Sam allowed himself an emotion he thought had died in that car accident with Wendy—

Hope.

He pulled into the driveway, parked the car, then got out and paused a moment in the driveway. The sound of children laughing, of Bandit barking, filled the air.

Life was good. In this moment, in this space. It was something he'd been trying to work on—learning to appreciate the small moments. After the dark days he and the kids had gone through, every small moment seemed like a miracle.

Sam allowed himself another smile, then circled around through the side gate to the backyard. "Sounds like you guys are having a great—"

His step faltered. For several long seconds, he was sure he was seeing things. But no, there was Katie, mud-spattered, her hair a wild jumble around her head, trying to clean up a spilled pot of red finger paint on the patio, while Henry and Libby ran barefoot through the grass, taking turns aiming the hose at each other and the dog.

"You're home!" Katie got to her feet, and brushed at her hair with the back of her hand, but all that did was smear a long streak of red paint across her temple. "That's so…great."

He tried not to laugh at the paint on her face, the clear relief in her features. He glanced around the yard again, and when he noticed one less person than he'd left here this morning, alarm bells went off in his head. "Where's Charity?"

"She's inside. She said she had to make a call."

He'd had a feeling Charity wasn't going to last long when he hired her, but he'd hoped she would at least make it until he found a suitable replacement. He'd have to talk to her about taking personal calls when he was paying her to watch his kids. "Did the kids dip her in paint and mud, too?"

"No. That was all my doing." Katie laughed. "After Libby and I finished working on her math, I got them the paints because they were complaining that they were bored, and I didn't want to just park them in front of the television. I asked Charity, and she said she thought it was a good idea to do a craft. Except I'm not exactly the crafty type." Katie gave him a sheepish grin. "Libby got paint on her hands and wanted to clean it off, but I didn't think you'd want her to do that in the bathroom sink, so I turned on the hose and..." She waved at the yard and grimaced.

Sam could read that look of being overwhelmed from a mile away. How many times had he felt totally over his head when it came to the kids? He'd been so used to putting it all into Wendy's hands, into letting her take the lead while he worked too many hours. When his wife was gone and the family who had hovered over him for the first two weeks after she died had left, Sam was left floundering, beleaguered and clueless.

A lot like Katie looked right now. Actually, she looked kind of cute with the mud and paint peppered all over her shirt and skirt. She'd kicked off the heels, and there was something about her bare feet on the grass that just seemed...sweet. A part of him wanted to just draw her against his chest and kiss that spot of paint right above her brow.

"Come on," he said to Katie, waving toward the door. "Why don't you go inside and clean up? I'll corral the wild beasts and then we'll all get some lunch."

"Are you sure? I can clean up this mess out here first."

"I can handle it. Don't worry."

Katie gave him a grateful smile, then headed inside. Sam watched her go for a moment, then dragged his gaze away from the intriguing woman crossing his yard.

The guilt washed over him again. He shouldn't be concentrating on anything other than his kids and his job right now. The kids needed him—needed a parent who kept his crap together, not one who got distracted by a pretty woman with mud on her face.

He headed for the kids, reached out and took the hose from Libby just before she turned it on her brother again. Both kids were dripping wet, sodden messes from head to toe. He was about to chastise them, when he looked down and realized something else.

Both kids were happy. Goofy grins filled their eyes and brightened their cheeks. "We had fun!" Libby said. "Can we do that again?"

Beside her, Henry nodded. His face was a blur of paint, half of it smeared by the water and now running crimson into his orange T-shirt. There was no trace of the somber, withdrawn boy who had appeared the day Sam had sat on the sofa and hugged his kids to him and told them Mommy was never coming home again.

He glanced over his shoulder at the house. It was amazing what a few hours of Katie in their lives could do. And that was a very good thing.

When the pain hit her, it hit her hard and fast.

For three days, Katie had been coming to Sam's

house for an hour or two at a time after school, to work with Libby. They had slowly winnowed down the pile of papers her teacher had sent home and she had nearly mastered her times tables. Then, when they were done with schoolwork, Katie would draw with both kids, a break Charity seemed to welcome, because the nanny immersed herself in her phone the second Katie appeared. Maybe because Charity was there a longer portion of the day, picking up Henry from storytime at the community center and watching him until Libby got home from school.

The kids had kept clamoring for more finger painting, so Katie had finally caved today. This time without the need to hose off in the yard.

Everything had been going fine until Charity announced she was quitting. She said she'd gotten a call back from a job at the mall, and was done being a nanny. She was gone two minutes later, leaving a stunned Katie alone with the kids for a half hour until Sam came home.

It was in that thirty minutes that things had changed. Maybe it was because it was just the three of them, or maybe the kids were starting to bond with Katie, but just as she was helping Libby mix up some purple paint, Henry had leaned in and put his head on Katie's arm.

A simple movement, really. She'd looked down and seen this little boy curving into her like he'd known her all his life. Then Libby turned to Katie and said, "Our mommy used to draw with us. I'm glad you do, too." A pause, then Libby's eyes met hers, wide and serious. "Are you gonna stay, Katie?"

Katie glanced up and saw Sam standing there, his face filled with a mixture of surprise and something unreadable.

Katie had scrambled out of the seat, made up an excuse about needing to clean up, then barreled toward the bathroom. One second she was soaping up her hands, and the next, a sharp fissure pierced her chest. Her breathing tightened, her heart crumpled into a fist and tears rushed into her eyes. She braced her still dirty hands on either side of the sink, heedless of the soapy, purplish drops puddling on the tile below.

She glimpsed her face in the mirror, looking harried and messy and so out of her normal buttoned-up world. *This is what a mom looks like*, her mind whispered, *and these are the kinds of things a mom does*.

Wham, the pain had hit her.

She wasn't a mom. She might never be a mom. The one chance she'd had to be a mother, her body had failed...no, *she* had failed. She'd lost the baby and all those hopes and dreams she'd had. What had made her think she could be here, around these kids, and not be reminded of that fact? Maybe she should tell Sam she couldn't tutor Libby. Or maybe she should just keep working here, because maybe it would force her to confront all those things she had run from.

Yeah, and considering how often in her life she'd confronted any of the things that bothered her, those chances were pretty slim.

A light rap sounded on the door. "You okay in there?" Sam's voice, warm and concerned. Just four words, but they seemed to ease the tightness in her chest.

Katie released her grip on the porcelain, drew in a breath, then nodded at her reflection. Another breath, then she could speak. "Yeah, just cleaning up."

"Okay. Just checking. I was afraid you might have

climbed out the window and run off, especially since Charity quit."

That made her laugh. "Nope, I haven't left. Not yet."

"That's good."

She paused, sensing Sam lingering outside the door. A moment later, she heard the fading sound of footsteps as he headed back down the hall. She finished rinsing and drying her hands, then emerged from the bathroom. In the kitchen, Sam was bent down, Libby standing before him, with one of the pictures she had painted that day in her hands. Libby's face held a hushed hesitancy.

Katie's chest squeezed. In a split second, she was eight years old again, standing in front of her mother with a test she'd brought home from school. Her first A in math class, decorated with a giant smiley face sticker. She'd wanted her mother to be as proud as Mrs. Walker had been, wanted to hear those same words *you did it, kiddo*.

"This is awesome, Libby Bear," Sam said to his daughter, taking the picture and pointing at the center. "I love the rainbow. And the flower."

Libby frowned. "I thought the flower was kinda messy."

Sam cupped his daughter's cheek. "It's not messy. It's perfect."

Katie waited for that echoing grin of pride to appear on Libby's face, for her to acknowledge she'd heard the words she wanted to. The *you did it, kiddo*.

Instead, Libby shook her head and stepped back. "It's not! It's messy!"

She yanked the picture out of her father's hand and dashed out of the kitchen. The screen door closed behind her with a hard slap. Sam watched her go, then let out a long sigh and slowly straightened.

He turned and saw Katie. "Sorry about that. Sometimes Libby is…" He shrugged. "I don't know. I honestly don't know."

"She's a great kid," Katie said. Because she didn't know what else to say. How to explain Libby's reaction to what seemed like a regular conversation between a father and daughter. A part of Katie wanted to run after Libby and tell her that parents who made a big deal out of every painted rainbow and hand-drawn flower weren't as common as she thought. That perfection wasn't all it was cracked up to be.

"Yeah, she is." Sam pivoted back to the bay window, watching his daughter through the glass. She toed back and forth on the swing, one foot dragging listlessly against the worn oval in the grass. The picture lay in a crumpled ball beneath her. "But she's been going through a lot and there are days…"

Katie's heart went out to him. He was so clearly worried about his children and desperate to reestablish a connection with them. It was as if there was this invisible wall between Sam and his children, one none of them knew how to scale. Katie was no expert in these matters, but she knew what it felt like to be on one side of that wall.

Before she could think about it, she put a hand on his shoulder. He was solid and warm beneath her palm. "She'll come around. You're a great dad."

"I'm *trying* to be a great dad," he said. "That's not the same thing."

Katie's hand dropped as she thought of her own mother. A woman too self-involved to be any kind of parent. Colton had shouldered most of that responsibility, an older brother thrust into a role he'd never asked for. Maybe it was because Katie had been the second surprise baby, an unwelcome intrusion into a life already strained by the birth of Colton a few years earlier. Her mother had never married, never made more than just enough to keep a roof over her head. "When it comes to kids, trying is important. And noticed."

He studied her for a moment. "Sounds like you have some experience with that."

Katie shrugged. "I had a mother who was...busy a lot."

"Back in Atlanta?" He crossed to the sink, filled two glasses with water and returned to hand one to her. "Did you grow up there?"

The past three days, their conversations had centered entirely around the kids. How Libby had done with her homework, whether they'd finished the book she had to read for reading class, things like that. The personal question threw Katie for a bit of a loop. "I've never really lived anywhere else, or had a chance to travel anywhere. Until now."

He chuckled. "I don't know if I'd call Stone Gap a destination city."

"It is for some people," she said quietly. Her brother, after all, had found happiness here. A life.

"I always vowed I was going to leave town when I grew up. But then I met Wendy and..." His gaze strayed to Libby. "Anyway, it's a great place to raise kids."

"I can see that," Katie said. "It has that Mayberry feel to it."

He laughed. "You say that like it's a bad thing."

She arched a brow.

He leaned against the wall and faced her. "Okay, yes, living in a small town does mean that everyone knows everything you do on any given day. But it also means that people are there when you need them, people like Della, who has been a huge help in the last year and a half."

Katie thought of the cold, sometimes scary neighborhoods where she'd grown up. There were years when they had moved so often she didn't know a single neighbor. "I bet that was nice."

"When I was a kid, there was this little old lady who lived next door to me. Mrs. Hanratty. She'd sit on her porch and watch the neighborhood kids walk to school, and on hot days, she'd be out there after school, giving us all ice-cold Popsicles. On really cold winter mornings, she'd have little cups of hot chocolate for us. She never had any kids of her own, and I think she kinda felt like all the kids around her were hers."

"I had a neighbor like that once," Katie said. "For a few months. Then we moved again."

"That had to be tough on you when you were growing up."

She shook her head, as if it hadn't been. "I had Colton. And I turned out okay."

"Maybe kids are more resilient than we think."

His gaze had gone to his daughter again, still drifting back and forth in the swing. Katie wanted to stay, wanted to help, but she was starting to feel those panicky feelings again. The ones that told her she had no business trying to be anything other than the tutor. "I should probably get going."

"Wait." Sam turned toward her. "I...uh, wanted to thank you."

She picked up her purse from the counter and hung it over her shoulder. "Thank me? For what?"

"For…everything." He waved a hand in a circle. "The house looks amazing, and I know Charity didn't do it, not unless I was paying her extra. I don't think I've ever seen the kitchen this clean. The whole house looks…cheery."

She shrugged and placed her hand on his arm. "It wasn't a big deal. I finished up with Libby, then decided to stay and clean up a little before we did the painting, which turned out to be a good thing, since Charity ended up quitting. Chalk it up to my CPA brain. I like things organized."

"It was a big deal. Everything you've done over these last few days has been." He shifted toward her, and Katie's hand dropped away. He was wearing a pale yellow button-down shirt and a dark green tie. A part of her wondered what it would be like to run that silky material between her fingers.

"You're really great with both kids," Sam went on. "You've got them learning, and doing art projects, and as soon as you leave, you're all they talk about. Libby told me she likes you, and she's never said that about any of the nannies I've hired. I know I hired you to be Libby's tutor, but would you consider—" he put up a hand, warding off her objections before she could voice them "—being the nanny? Just until I have time to find someone permanent, because I know you aren't staying here for very long. My schedule is flexible, Libby has school, Henry has storytime and sometimes other activities at the community center, so it will really only be for a few hours a day. Heck, you've been here that long almost every day, and done more than Charity did in a month."

She flashed back to that moment in the bathroom. Of how being around these kids, seeing how attached they were getting to her, had hurt, deep in her chest. Could she deal with this all day? Every day?

Then she looked out the window at Libby, a sad little girl drifting back and forth in the swing, and she saw...

Herself.

What if someone had stepped in when Katie was little, in all those hours she'd sat at home on the sofa, waiting for Colton to get home from softball practice or her mother to come home from work? What if someone had been there to bake cookies and spill finger paints and fix broken teddy bears? What if someone had been there to say that A on the math test was amazing? Would it have made a difference?

"I don't have much experience," Katie said.

"You've been here every day for three days, and even Charity told me you've been great. I know the kids can be...overwhelming sometimes. Especially when they're armed with finger paints and a hose." He grinned.

Sam's smile was a little lopsided, with a slight dimple in his left cheek. She liked his smile. Liked it a lot. Wouldn't mind seeing it more often. And if he was going to be popping in throughout the day to help with the kids...

Was she seriously considering this job?

She didn't have anything to rush back to, no fire in her belly to get back to Atlanta. "I could maybe extend my time here," she said. "So the kids don't have a lot of change in a short period of time."

"So you'll take the job?" Sam asked. "And be the nanny?"

Her gaze traveled again to Libby, then to Henry, dwarfed by an oversize chair in the living room. He had a stuffed dog clutched to his chest, and his knees drawn up against him, while he watched TV. There was a smudge of finger paint on his cheek, like a royal blue fingerprint.

That smudge tugged at something deep inside Katie, something she hadn't even been sure existed until she walked into this house and met these children. This man.

"Okay," she said. "I'll do it."

## Chapter Five

Sam noticed the flowers first. The window boxes, neglected for a long, long time, now bloomed with pink and white geraniums. A slight breeze moved the petals back and forth, almost as if they were waving. The terra-cotta planters that flanked the front porch had also been refilled, with more of the same kind of flowers cascading over the edges.

Sam fingered one of the flowers, thinking it had been ages since he'd seen anything growing in his yard. The flowers looked happy, bright. Hopeful.

He'd spent six frenzied hours at work today, zipping from client to client, answering calls and sending emails in the snippets of time he had between meetings. He'd had three showings to potential renters for the mall property, but none of them had made an offer. Since it was Katie's first day as nanny, Sam cut out early and grabbed some take-out Chinese food on his way home.

He'd never expected to see flowers. He hadn't realized how much he'd missed that kind of thing until he saw the geraniums. They were a change. A good change.

Then the guilt hit him, coming from left field like a rogue wave. Should he be enjoying the flowers another woman had planted on Wendy's porch? When his late wife would undoubtedly rather he worry about the kids, his job, everything else?

Or was it just that he was finding himself more and more drawn to Katie, and the guilt over having feelings for another woman was eating away at him? He had loved Wendy, Lord knew he had loved her, and he didn't want to tarnish the memory of a good wife and good mother by moving on too soon.

Best just to focus on the kids. That was what Wendy would want, too, he was sure.

He opened the front door and heard Libby's voice. He quieted his steps as he headed down the hall, trying to catch the gist of what she was saying.

"And then Kayla says that she wants to wear her pink shoes tomorrow, so I think I'm gonna wear my pink shoes, because Kayla is my best friend, and we both love pink," Libby said, her voice rising with excitement.

"That'll be awesome," Katie said. "Does Kayla like playing soccer, too?"

Sam lingered against the wall, watching his daughter, her head bent over a drawing she was working on as she talked. This normal moment, missed for so long in his house, was like seeing the flowers. Bright, happy. Hopeful.

"Kayla doesn't like soccer as much as me," Libby said. "But she said maybe she'll join the soccer team, if I do it, too."

"I used to play soccer in high school." Katie handed Libby a red crayon, then turned to Henry and slid a straw into his juice box. He climbed onto the chair beside them and started scribbling on a second coloring book. "My brother was a really great soccer player and he taught me all kinds of awesome moves."

"He did? Can you..." Libby hesitated, then looked up at Katie. "Can you teach me them, too?"

Katie laughed. "I don't know if I remember them, but I bet my brother does. Maybe I can have him come over tomorrow afternoon and show you. He's a firefighter."

That piqued Henry's interest. "A firefighter?"

"Yup. And if it's okay with your dad, I can take you guys down to the station and let you see the fire trucks."

The whole exchange was so normal, so uncolored by the sadness that had hung over this house like a heavy drape. Coloring books and soccer and visits to the firehouse. Regular family stuff, the kind of thing so many people took for granted.

Until it was gone.

Sam didn't know whether to cheer or cry. He'd wanted this...normalcy for his kids for so long. But it came attached to another woman, one he thought about way too often.

Sam pushed off from the wall and went into the kitchen. "Hey, a trip to the fire station sounds great to me. I want to go, too. As long as I get to toot the horn on the big truck."

Katie turned toward him and smiled, the kind of smile that said she was happy to see him. "I think you are a little too old for that."

Sam grinned. "A boy is never too old to do that, isn't that right, Henry?"

Henry nodded, clambered down from the chair, then

plowed into Sam's legs. He held on tight, while Sam ran a hand through his son's scraggly brown locks.

Libby stayed at the table, coloring and mostly ignoring Sam. The wall between himself and his daughter sometimes seemed impossible to scale. The moment of hopefulness began to fade.

Sam lifted the Chinese food up and away from Henry's now reaching arms. "Hold on a second, buddy. Let me put this—"

Katie was there, taking the bag from him. She had this uncanny ability to read his mind. "Here, let me help."

He smiled at her, then hefted his son into his arms. Henry settled against Sam's chest like he was made for that space. "Thank you," Sam whispered.

She smiled. "It was nothing."

But Sam looked at his daughter, coloring a picture of a farm, and his son, who was grinning from ear to ear, and disagreed. Things weren't perfect, but they were a sight better than they had been before. The house was clean, the kids were happy and engaged. There was an air of...hope around everything that he hadn't felt in a long time.

Sam lowered Henry to the floor. "Hey, buddy, go finish your picture for me, okay?"

Henry nodded and went back to the table. Katie was laying out the Chinese food on the counter. She added a pile of plates and silverware, then stepped back and brushed her hands together. "Well, I should go," she said. "Same time tomorrow?"

She'd done the same thing every day this week, leaving right after he got home. He felt like he barely knew her, and wanted to get to know her. Not just as a tutor for his daughter, but as a woman. He wanted to know what it was about her that was changing his life and breathing life into the dark spaces.

It was the flowers. Those damned flowers.

Sam caught Katie's hand as she started to pass by him. Like the first time they'd touched, an electric jolt ran through him. Her lips parted and her eyes widened, and he wondered if she'd felt the same thing. "Stay for dinner?"

She grinned. "I already eat lunch here every day after I pick Henry up from the community center. Feeding me wasn't part of the deal."

"Consider it a tip." He returned her smile.

"But the kids…" She glanced over at the table, where Libby and Henry were back to coloring again.

"Surely want you to stay as much as I do." Had he just said that out loud? To a woman other than his wife? It was for the kids, he told himself, only for the kids' benefit. He turned toward the table. "Hey, guys, do you want Katie to stay for dinner?"

"Yes!" Libby dropped her crayon onto the page and ran over to Katie. "Can you sit next to me? I wanna sit next to you."

Katie laughed. "Okay, okay. With an invitation like that, how can I say no?"

The four of them divvied up the Chinese food, then settled around the kitchen table. As they ate, Libby began to open up, nudged by strategic questions from Katie, about her day at school, about the decision to wear pink shoes with Kayla the next day, about the cool dog they saw at the park. Bandit sat beside the table, tail swishing against the floor, hoping for a dropped morsel.

When the take-out boxes were empty and the last crab Rangoon eaten by Henry, Sam gathered the plates and got to his feet. "You kids can either help with the dishes or—" he gave them a grin "—play in the yard."

A half second later, both Libby and Henry had escaped to the backyard, with Bandit hot on their heels. Katie started the hot water and loaded the few plates and pieces of silverware into the sink. "That was great Chinese food. Thank you for inviting me to stay."

"Thank you for staying."

She laughed. "You had me at Moo Shu Pork."

He slipped into place beside her and started drying as she washed. They fell into an easy rhythm, working together seamlessly. Wendy had always done the dishes alone, preferring the time to think, she'd said. It wasn't until he was on his own that he'd stayed in the kitchen longer than the time it took to finish a meal. But this was nice, working beside Katie on something as simple as washing a few plates. It felt odd, but also nice. He wasn't sure how to process that, so he didn't. He just kept on doing the dishes.

"I can't remember the last time we ate off of real plates," he said, slipping the blue-rimmed dinner plate into the cabinet. "I've pretty much stuck to whatever was disposable and quick."

"I'm sorry. I shouldn't have—"

He put a hand over hers, and that connection hit him again. "Stop apologizing. I'm glad you did it. It's about time all of us started...living again. Like a normal family."

She stiffened at that, and he wondered what he'd said that had caused the sudden coolness between them. Before he could ask, she had shut off the water and pulled the drain plug. "Well, that's it. I guess I'll see you tomorrow."

The kids were still playing outside, with the dog

chasing around them and barking. The sun was starting to ease behind the horizon, and soon it would be dark and the kids would be inside and this moment would be lost. Sam wasn't sure if he would be better off holding on to it or letting go.

Katie was gathering her purse and getting ready to leave. Sam stood there like a fool, so new to dating again that he wasn't quite sure how to go about it, or if he even should. She was the nanny, after all, and it wasn't a good idea. But she'd filled his chest with something that had been missing for a long, long time, and he wasn't prepared to let that go just yet.

"I saw the flowers," he said, just as she waved and started down the hall.

"The flowers? Oh, yeah." Katie turned back. "I hope you're not mad. I thought it would be a great project for the kids. And it's spring and, well, flowers just go with spring and…" She grimaced. "I presumed too much. Those are your planters and I shouldn't have just done that without asking first."

"They're…perfect."

"I'm glad you like them." She fiddled with her keys for a moment. "Well, I should go."

"Wait. Please." He came down the hall, where the light was dimmer and Katie's features seemed almost iridescent. He shifted closer to her, inhaling the light floral fragrance she wore. Her eyes widened, her lips parted and the desire that had been simmering inside him for hours began nudging him forward, until a fraction of space separated them.

"I'm glad you like the flowers," she said again, but her gaze lingered on his lips, and her body shifted ever so slightly in his direction.

"I do. Very much." He wasn't talking about the impatiens or geraniums or whatever the hell they were. He was talking about this woman who had come into his life and, in a handful of days, changed damned near everything. Things he wasn't sure should be changed, but he seemed powerless to stop any of it. Maybe because deep down inside, a part of him craved this change, craved...

Her.

Sam reached up and traced the side of her cheek, along the line of her jaw, holding her gaze with his own. Something so simple, yet so intense, with her brown eyes locked on his and their breaths mingling in the small space.

Then before he could think about what he was doing, Sam leaned in and kissed Katie. A short kiss, a momentary touch, but as he began to pull back, something pushed him forward again. He cradled the back of her head, she let out a soft, sweet sound and he opened his mouth against hers.

She curved into him, with her body, with her mouth, with everything. Desire roared through Sam, not just for a woman, but for this woman, this intriguing, captivating woman. He'd been alone for so, so long. In all that time, no one had tempted him like Katie did.

There was a sound outside, a shriek of laughter from Libby, a loud bark from Bandit. Sam jerked to his senses and pulled back. What was he doing? He'd taken his focus off the kids, off the most important thing in his life. Guilt rolled through him. What about Wendy? What about her memory? Was he doing his wife a disservice by kissing another woman?

Then he saw Katie, her cheeks still flushed, and all he could think about was kissing her again. How long was he going to wait to start his life over again?

"I'm out of practice, and I know I just did all this in the wrong order, with kissing you first and…" It was like he was fourteen again and asking Mary Sue Matlin out on a date. He was nervous and stammering and a jumbled mess. "Anyway, I'd really like to ask you out. For dinner, for drinks, for…whatever."

Hesitation flickered on her face. "I…I don't think I should."

"Because you're the nanny or because you're not interested?" He was pretty sure he'd read interest in that kiss. A whole lot of interest. Or maybe she was feeling just as conflicted as he was.

"Because…I'm complicated." She gave him a half smile, then reached up and touched his cheek. It was a flutter of a touch, just a second, but it warmed him. The smile faltered on her face and she stepped back. "I'll see you tomorrow, Sam."

Then she was gone, and Sam was left in his hall, wondering what she'd meant, and why the answer intrigued him so much.

"So, are you going to tell me?"

Katie looked up from her sandwich and grinned at her brother. They were sitting in the Good Eatin' Café, grabbing a late night snack, a few days after she'd started working full-time for Sam. She hadn't even been that hungry, but once she heard Colton order a grilled cheese sandwich, she couldn't resist getting one, too. Plus, it was always good to see her brother. Grounding, in a way. "Tell you what?"

"What are you doing? Taking on a nanny job for Sam, going around with that goofy grin on your face—"

"I do not have a goofy grin on my face."

"You do indeed. Every time I mention Sam's name that goofy grin pops up, like a balloon in a box."

She dropped her gaze to the plate. Was it that obvious that she was interested in Sam Millwright? Was that why he had kissed her? Why he had asked her out? Because she was as obvious as an infatuated teenager whenever he walked in the room? "I'm his children's nanny," Katie said, "nothing more."

Except she was 100 percent sure kissing Sam was not in her job description. Try as she might to pretend that kiss hadn't happened, it hung in the air every time she was at his house.

Colton had picked up on it several times during the last week when she'd seen him. He'd also latched onto the fact that she had extended her "vacation," although she hadn't told him the real reason why she wasn't going back to Atlanta yet.

"Remind me again, you're working as a nanny because…?" Colton prompted.

"Colton, this isn't a remake of the *Sound of Music*. I'm not there to marry the handsome bachelor dad." She shook her head. "Can we change the subject, please?"

"Okay, then let's talk about…weddings." He grinned.

She groaned. "I just told you. I'm not marrying anyone. For Pete's sake, all I did was take a job—"

"Not you. Me. Rachel and I are planning our wedding. If you ask me, the big day can't come soon enough. I love that woman like crazy." Now a goofy grin spread across Colton's face, the kind that said he was madly in love.

A flicker of envy ran through Katie. That was crazy. She didn't need or want a relationship right now. All relationships did was bring disappointment. Colton had gotten lucky—that one-in-a-million chance of finding someone who wasn't going to break your heart—but that didn't mean there was another one-in-a-million out there for Katie. Best to just not get involved at all.

Even with sexy widowers who had a tender touch and a deep voice. Who also happened to be amazing kissers. Her mind wandered back to that moment in the hall, to the way he had touched her face, made her melt, then—

"I'm so happy for you," Katie said. "Really."

"Since there's going to be a wedding in my near future, I wanted to ask… Are you going to be here for that?"

"Of course. You know I'd come back to Stone Gap for your wedding, even if I have to wear an ugly bridesmaid's dress."

Colton didn't laugh. His face was sober, serious. "I meant stay here. Don't go back to Atlanta. Live in Stone Gap. You already have a job, after all."

Katie was halfway to another bite and stopped. "Stay here? I only arrived a little over a week ago. I'm on vacation, not relocating."

"A vacation that now doesn't have any discernible end date, a vacation where you are working as a nanny? What kind of person takes on a job when they're on vacation?"

*Someone who wants to keep too busy to think. Someone who doesn't actually know how to unwind. Someone who is a little lost and trying to buy some time before making a decision.* "Sam was desperate," Katie said instead. "I told him I'd help him. It's only a few hours a day and it was a temporary thing."

"Uh-huh. You do know you've never been able to lie to me, right?"

"I'm not lying."

"Then answer me this, Abe Lincoln." He gestured toward her purse, closed and sitting on the bench seat beside her. "Your phone isn't out on the table. You're not checking it every half second. You're not pausing every five minutes to call someone back or shoot off an email or anything else. You're completely unplugged, and you are *never* completely unplugged. You, my sister, are a workaholic, who isn't working."

Katie fiddled with her silverware and finally pushed the remains of her sandwich away. "I sort of came to an agreement with my boss that I wasn't going to work there anymore."

"Wait. You got *fired*? *You?*"

"Not fired–fired. It was a mutual decision." Of sorts. He arched a brow.

"It's a long story." One she'd managed to avoid telling, since Colton worked long hours and was often with Rachel.

"I've got all night." Colton leaned back and draped his arm over the vinyl edge of the bench. "And a running tab for decaf here."

"Have I told you lately that you are a total pain in the ass?"

Colton checked his watch. "Uh, not in the last thirty minutes."

That made her laugh and eased the wall in her mind. Maybe it *was* time to talk about everything. After all, not talking about what bothered her hadn't helped. Bottling it all up had, in fact, led to a volcanic explosion at work. Hence the not fired–fired events and the temporary nanny job and the muddle in her mind. Not to mention that kiss with Sam. Whatever that had been and whatever that had meant.

"I don't even know where to start," Katie said. "Or how to explain what happened."

Colton reached across the table and took her hand.

His was bigger, stronger, more solid. The same as he
had been when she'd been three and scared of monsters
in the closet, and when he walked with her into every
new school, and when he'd been there with a hug when
her heart had been broken in tenth grade. Colton had
been there every single time, with his goofy smile and
his big strong hands and his patient gaze. "Just start
with why you came to Stone Gap."

"I was running away." Tears burned her eyes and
she shrugged, trying to pass it off as nothing. But the
pain surged to the surface all over again, like a wave
she couldn't hold back. "I couldn't stay there one more
day and be reminded of…"

"Of your job?" he finished, when her voice trailed off.

"Of…" She drew in a breath, held it, then let it out.
She'd told no one about what had happened, and sud-
denly, the burden seemed too heavy, the ache too deep.
"The baby."

Colton blinked. He sat back again and let out a low
whistle. "Did you say *baby*?"

She nodded. And now that she had said that word, the
rest came tumbling out, breaking past all those strong-
holds she'd put in place to keep her from having to feel
anything. Really, all it had done was keep her stuck in
place. She wanted to move forward, wanted to put it all
far, far behind her. "Remember I was dating that guy
Leonard? Well, one night we were drunk and in a rush,
and I thought he had put protection on, but he hadn't,
and… I got pregnant."

Her brother's gaze dropped to her belly. "Are you…?
Did you…?"

The tears spilled over her eyelashes and trailed down
her cheeks. She was back in the doctor's office all over
again, knowing what he was going to say before he even

spoke a word. She'd known it the minute her body began to betray her, that the dream she'd had was gone before she had a chance to hold on to it. "I lost the baby. Ten weeks in, and I lost it. I was just getting used to the idea, and as crazy as it sounds, looking forward to having my own family. I know I always said I never wanted to have kids, not after living with Mom, but you know, I really thought—" her voice caught, but she kept pushing the words out "—that I would be a good mother."

"Of course you would have been," Colton said. "Hell, you were half mother to me, Piglet."

"Me? I was the annoying tagalong. You were the one who was there for me all the time."

"Because you were the one who always worried about me. You still do."

"You're a big grown man." She waved off his words. "I don't worry about you."

He grinned. "Liar. I have some text messages that say the opposite."

It was true. She did text him from time to time to make sure he was okay. Even more in the year after he'd lost two friends at the scene of a fire. For a while there she'd been pretty worried that Colton wouldn't come out of the depression that had swept over him after the accident. But he had, and now he was back doing the job he loved, and moving forward with Rachel. "Those texts are just me ensuring you're still alive so I'll get a decent Christmas present this year."

"What, you didn't like the Scrooge and Marley action figures I sent you last year? Or the subscription to the NASCAR magazine the year before?"

"Not as much as I bet you enjoyed the *Dating for Dummies* book I sent you."

He mocked offense. "I'll have you know that book is

a godsend. After all, I'm getting married. Which means I'm going to have an excuse to see you in some lime-green bridesmaid dress with poufy sleeves."

"I've changed my mind. I'll only wear an ugly brides-maid dress if it's to attend your funeral." She grinned. The moment of levity eased the sadness, dried up Katie's tears and gave her a moment to breathe. "How do you do that?" she asked Colton. "I can be telling you the saddest story ever and somehow, you make me laugh and make it all seem…not so bad."

"It's my secret power." He signaled for some more coffee, and waited to speak again until after the wait-ress had topped off their mugs. "I'm sorry about the baby, Katie."

"It's okay. It wasn't meant to be." The platitude didn't give her any comfort. It was simply a way to fill the hole in the conversation.

"You would have been a great mom and you will be someday," Colton said again. "A really great mom."

"Almost as great a mom as you were."

He grinned. "You weren't too much of a brat, so it was easy." He took a sip of coffee, then leaned closer. "So how did all that lead to you not exactly being fired from your job?"

She told him about the meltdown, about the cli-ents they had lost, about the argument with her boss. "Around that same time, you texted me, asking me again to come to Stone Gap, so…here I am."

"I'm glad you are. I think you needed this town more than you knew. It's been good for me, Katie, and I'm sure it'll be good for you." He ate a french fry. "I still don't understand how that all led to you being Sam's nanny, though."

She circled the rim of her mug with her finger a few

times before answering. "I needed to keep busy, so I wouldn't keep thinking about everything. Della told me he needed a tutor, and I thought, great, I could work an hour or two a day and make a little money. Then his babysitter up and quit on him and he was desperate and…"

"And you took the opportunity to keep even busier."

She nodded. "You know me well."

"I share your DNA. That makes me an expert." He ate another couple fries, dunking them in ketchup before they disappeared in his mouth. Colton had the appetite of ten men, but worked out enough that he never seemed to gain an ounce. "So, are you planning on doing any actual vacationing while you are here?"

"If I vacation, I'll think, and I'm trying not to do that."

"Exactly why you should do it." He covered her hand again. "Take it from someone who spent a long time trying not to think about my biggest screwups. It's not until you finally look at the elephant in the room that you can figure out how to get it outside again."

She laughed. "I think that is the most convoluted piece of advice I've ever heard."

"Confucius say it's wise and profound. Because it's coming from your older brother. So you'd be smart to listen. And to have dessert with me."

"Why should I have dessert with you?"

"Because dessert, dear sister, makes everything better." Then he ordered pie, and told her a bunch of funny stories about the firehouse, and before Katie knew it, Colton had worked his magic again. Rescuing her one more time.

## Chapter Six

Sam got up extra early, got Libby off to school, Henry off to a morning of crafts and stories at the community center, then rushed through his day like a man on fire. Every time he glanced at the clock, he was hoping it was noon, so that he could finagle some kind of excuse to stop by the house.

Because from the minute he'd woken up, his every other thought had revolved around Katie. Her smile. The way she touched him. How insanely amazing it had been to kiss her the other day. How she had turned down his dinner invitation.

*Because I'm complicated.*

Her response had left him confused. Okay, so he was a guy, and what women wanted and what they meant when they said things like that pretty much left him confused all the time. Still, he wanted to know what she meant. And why she had kissed him, yet turned him down.

Was it wrong to look forward to coming home to her? To think about kissing her? Holding her?

For several days, he'd tried to concentrate on work. He'd sold two commercial properties—a vacant warehouse outside of Stone Gap and a small office building in a neighboring town, which had put him in Hank's good graces. But all that work hadn't done much to keep him from thinking about Katie.

He turned his gaze to the blue, blue sky above. Wisps of clouds dotted the vast cornflower-colored canvas, seeming to promise anything was possible. That answers were there, if only he asked the right questions.

*What would Wendy want?*

It was a question Sam had asked himself every day since his wife had died. Would she want him to move on? Or would she want him to wait, to keep that space in his heart reserved a little longer?

"I wish I knew," he whispered to the sky. Because as wrong as it was to feel this happy coming home, there were many times when it felt so very right.

So there he was, in his own driveway a little after twelve, even though he had an appointment across town at one. Five minutes, tops, then he'd get back in the car and go back to work. Just a quick visit to say hi to Henry after his morning at the community center. The program had been a godsend—keeping Henry busy and playing with other kids, but not putting the pressure on him to talk like school would.

"I'm home," Sam called as he walked in the door. Something smelled good inside the house. There was music playing on the sound system in the dining room, and everything seemed to sparkle and shine. Sam hadn't realized how much he missed coming home to a house that was an actual home until these last couple days.

Katie was in the kitchen, mixing some kind of batter in a bowl. Henry was sitting at one of the kitchen bar stools, holding a big wooden spoon. Katie had her hair up in one of those clip things, which left a few long brown tendrils in tempting curls along the valleys of her neck. Today, she had on a pair of jeans that hugged her hips and outlined some very, very nice curves. Her bright green V-neck T-shirt sported a logo for the Green Bay Packers and a reminder of the four Super Bowl championships they'd won.

She glanced up as he entered the kitchen, and a bright smile burst on her face. "Hi."

"Hi. Sorry. I wasn't checking on you, just stopping by on my way to a meeting."

"You're just in time. Henry and I are busy making cookies to give to the firefighters later today. Isn't that right, buddy? Here, your turn to mix." She turned the bowl in front of Henry, and he dug in with this spoon for one quick flip of the batter.

"Cookies!" Henry said, and held up his spoon. "Daddy have some?"

Sam's throat closed, but he worked a smile to his face that hopefully didn't say every time he heard Henry speak it damned near turned him into a baby. "Maybe later. I have to go back to work in a few minutes."

Henry's bright features dimmed. He went back to stirring the batter, but his movements were listless, slow. "Okay."

Sam had been here for ten seconds and already disappointed his son. He shot a glance at Katie, who gave him a sympathetic smile.

"How about I meet you guys at the fire station later?" Sam did a mental rundown of his schedule and figured if nothing ran over its allotted time, he should be able to be there on time.

"That would be great," Katie said. "The kids would love it if you were there."

"I'm gonna play with the fire truck!" Henry spread his arms wide, sending a spray of batter onto the kitchen floor.

"Hey, let's keep the dough in the bowl, buster." Katie took the spoon out of Henry's hands, then grabbed a paper towel to wipe up the mess. Sam reached for one at the same time, his arm brushing against Katie's shoulder.

It was a small touch, a whisper, really, but it sent a shock wave through Sam. Katie's gaze darted to his, held for a moment, then Henry ran over and tried to climb onto Sam's back. That was enough to break the spell, to keep him from leaning in for another amazing kiss with Katie. Later, Sam promised himself, there would be time for that. He'd make sure of it.

"Let me clean this up," Sam said, swinging Henry off his back with one arm, and cradling him against his waist. "And let this monkey here help me."

Henry giggled. "I's a boy!"

"Monkey boy." Sam tweaked Henry's nose, then handed him half the paper towel. "Help Daddy clean up."

Henry did as he was told, taking great pride in swiping up the clumps of batter, then dumping the mess into the trash. While the boys did that, Katie finished mixing the dough and adding in the chips, then she turned to get a stack of cookie sheets out of the drawer beneath the stove.

Henry was already gone, running off to play with whatever toy had caught his eye, the dog hot on his heels, and Sam was left alone in the kitchen with Katie, with a very appealing view of her rear.

Damn. This nanny thing was adding complications he hadn't expected. Like every five seconds he was wondering how he could get her alone. "You, uh, need some help?" he said.

"I've got it." She straightened, and laid two cookie sheets on the counter.

"I didn't even know I had those."

"And here you struck me as the baker type." She gave him a grin.

"My baking skills extend to once, and only once, slicing up one of those logs of dough and then forgetting about it."

"You forgot about them? What happened?" She scooped up balls of dough with a spoon and began sliding them onto the cookie sheet.

"Let's just say I was airing the house out for three days and going through a couple cans of oven cleaner. I'm not exactly domesticated." He slipped into place beside her and picked up the second tablespoon beside the bowl. "Do I just put it on there? None of that spray stuff first?" He'd seen Wendy spray that nonstick stuff on pretty much everything before she cooked.

"Nope. They'll spread too much if you do that. Just try to make sure all the cookies are about the same size so they bake evenly."

He did as she said, working at a slower pace than Katie, who seemed to have some kind of magic scooping and dumping skills. They each filled one cookie sheet, three across, four down. "This is nice," he said as they worked. "I've never done this before."

"Your wife must have made cookies all the time."

He steeled himself. In the months after his wife died,

every mention of her had felt like ripping open an old wound. But this time…not so much. Talking about her felt like he was warming himself by a familiar fire.

"Wendy was one of those moms who colored the pictures and decorated the rooms and baked the cookies, but the kitchen was her domain, and she was pretty particular about it." A bittersweet smile crossed his lips. If there was one thing his late wife had excelled at, it was being a mother. It was as if she had been born for that singular purpose. She had loved the kids, and been so close to them it was almost as if they were three parts of one person. She would have loved Katie, the way she handled the kids, got Henry to talk, encouraged Libby with her schoolwork. "Wendy was great, she really was. I don't want to make it sound like she was anything but a great mother."

"No wonder the kids miss her so much."

And he was a poor substitute for the mother they had lost. He didn't bake cookies or do crafts or remember their favorite bedtime story. He did the only thing he knew how to do— he worked and kept the bills paid. But in the long, long months since their mother had died, he had realized how much more his kids needed. They needed the cookies and the finger paints and the silly jokes. For the thousandth time, he was grateful that Katie had shown up on his doorstep. "Do they talk about their mother with you?" he asked.

She turned and slid the cookie sheets into the oven, then set the timer. "Libby has. She tells me stories about your wife. About the books she read her, the way she liked her ice cream, the times she took her to the park."

Sam leaned against the counter and let out a sigh. Libby was the oldest and had taken the loss of her mother the hardest. His heart broke for the days ahead—

the proms, the first heartbreaks, the wedding day, when Libby would need her mother and her mother wouldn't be there. Would he be able to fill those gaps? "My kids miss her a lot. It's been tough."

"I'm no expert, but they seem to be doing okay," Katie said. "You're a great dad, Sam."

He scoffed. "I'm a fair to middling dad. I'm trying to do better than I did before. When Wendy was alive, I worked too many hours and left too much on her shoulders. Then she died, and I still worked too many hours. Mostly because I didn't want to think about losing her. I didn't want to come home to an empty house. So I left the kids with a nanny and I worked too much..."

"And became even more distant."

"Yeah. It's like my kids grew up when I wasn't looking. I used to know Libby's favorite song and what kind of cereal she liked. Now I'm just trying to keep my head above water." He grabbed a sponge and wiped up the dusting of flour on the counter. "After the last nanny quit and I lost my job, I was here all the time, doing everything. The problem was, I don't know how to do everything. I don't remember that Libby likes the edges cut off her sandwiches or that Henry needs a certain stuffed animal to sleep with. And I sure as hell don't do anything the way Wendy did."

"Who says you have to do things the same way? And for the record, I don't think anyone knows how to do everything when it comes to raising a family. Last I checked, they didn't hand out instruction manuals in the delivery room."

He chuckled. "I think they should."

"Heck, I think they should give everyone one at high school graduation." She turned back to the cabinet, giving him that appealing view of her behind again, then straightened and put two wire racks on the counter. Another thing he didn't know he owned. "Did you eat lunch? I'm no chef, but I did make a pretty spectacular turkey-and-cheese sandwich for Henry."

"If I can take it to go. I have a meeting at one."

She got the ingredients out of the fridge, then put the sandwich together, sliced it on the diagonal and handed it to him on top of a paper towel. "Here you go."

He chuckled lightly. "You divided it on the angle. My mom used to cut my sandwiches like that. Is that why you do?"

"My mom didn't do much sandwich making in my house." Katie's gaze dropped to the sink. "Colton pretty much did all that stuff."

"Colton? Really?" Sam couldn't imagine the firefighter cutting sandwiches for his little sister. He remembered Colton telling him that his childhood had been tough, but he'd never gone into detail.

"Our mother...wasn't around much, and I never knew my father," Katie said. "Colton did a lot of the things she should have done."

That made Sam admire Katie even more. She had fit in so easily in this house, better than any of the previous nannies. "So how is it that you knew just what to do to get my kids to relax and open up and laugh for the first time in forever?"

"Easy," Katie said. "I just did the opposite of what my mother did."

"Well, you're doing a fabulous job. Even if you are a Packer fan." He gestured toward the shirt.

"Let me guess. You're more of a Pats fan. Or the Colts."

"Bears all the way, baby." He grinned, then grinned some more when the "baby" made her blush.

"A Bears fan? I knew you were too good to be true."
She grinned back at him.

He took a step closer, his sandwich forgotten. "You
thought I was too good to be true?"

"For maybe a blip of a second."

"And yet you won't go out with me?"

"It's…complicated."

He stared down into her eyes and thought he could
spend hours right here. "You keep saying that, but I
don't see anything complicated about you, Katie. So
what do you say? Dinner tonight after the fire station?
I can ask Della to take the kids for a couple hours."

"I'm not dressed for dinner and—"

"Where we are going, you don't need anything but
what you have on right now." He placed his palm on
the counter, a millimeter from hers. He wanted to kiss
her again, wanted to do a whole lot more than that, but
Henry was twenty feet away, playing with his trucks,
and the cookies were nearly done, and…

Sam didn't want to screw it up. He was new to dating again, not even sure he should be dating, but un-
able to resist this woman. The last thing he wanted to
do was rush it. Maybe that was why she had said no
yesterday. Because he had gone and kissed her first,
asked her out second.

"So, it's a date?" he said. Was it? Even he wasn't sure.

She hesitated. "I'm not looking for anything permanent, you know."

"I'm not asking you to." Now he did reach up and
brush one of those stray tendrils off her cheek. "It's just
a date, Katie, not a lifetime commitment."

*Just a date, not a lifetime commitment.*
Uh-huh. If that was so, then why was Katie so ner-

vous? It wasn't like she'd never dated before. And whatever happened with Sam would be temporary. Despite how wonderful it felt to be in his arms, and how the way he looked at her made everything inside her warm. Eventually, she was going back to Atlanta, and pursuing anything with Sam would be a mistake.

"Is this how I do it?" Libby asked, drawing Katie's attention back to the present, to her job. As the nanny, not the girlfriend.

"Almost," Katie said. She took the needle from Libby's hand and slid it near the edge of the bear's torn head. Katie had bought a sewing kit last night, and given the small basket of needles and thread to Libby, then taught her how to use it. Katie had done half the reattachment, and then showed Libby how to sew the two pieces together. "You want little stitches, so it won't show."

"Like this?" Libby slid the needle into the faux fur, then wriggled it out the other side.

"Exactly like that. Great job, Libby."

The little girl beamed. She was snuggled up against Katie on the couch, while Henry sat at their feet, building something out of blocks. While Katie was feeling like a fraud. These kids and Sam all looked at her like she was some kind of maternal wonder. All she could hear in her head was the doctor's voice telling her she had lost her baby.

The doctor had added all the normal platitudes— *these things happen, nothing you could do*—but deep down inside, Katie was sure if she had slept more or eaten better or worked less, none of it would have happened.

She was already growing attached to these kids, to this town, and that was a dangerous thing. She needed to get back to Atlanta, back to accounting, where all the credits and debits added up in neat little rows. Then maybe she could rid herself of this aching need for something she couldn't have.

"I'm glad we're fixing George, 'cuz he's my favorite bear," Libby said.

Katie cleared her throat and forced herself back to the present. "Why is he your favorite?"

"My mommy bought him when I was just a baby. She said it was my first toy." Libby stroked the bear's head. Tears glistened in her eyes. "I let Henry play with it sometimes, but it's my bear."

"George is a great bear. And it's really nice of you to let your brother play with it, too."

Libby slid another stitch in, a second, a third, before she spoke again. "Do you think my mommy is mad at me for breaking George?"

These were the moments when Katie wished she could call in a relief nanny, one who would know what to say to these heartbroken kids. "Oh, sweetie, no. Moms know that kids argue sometimes. She's not mad at all. And I bet she's really proud to see you fixing George. You're doing a great job." The stitches were even and tight. Libby had gotten the hang of sewing pretty quickly.

The praise seemed to warm Libby even more. She worked hard on the bear, her lips pursed in concentration, while Katie gave her little pointers. Katie glanced at the two kids, and for a second wondered if this was what it would have been like if she had gotten married and had kids of her own.

Would she have been the kind of mother who made pancakes and bought teddy bears and tied hair bows? Or would she have been distracted and busy and absent? Would she have had the best of intentions to be an involved, hands-on mom, or would she have let work take over her days?

Would her baby have had her brown hair and eyes, or ended up with Leonard's black hair?

Katie's hand strayed to her abdomen, to the empty cavern there that almost seemed to ache sometimes. She'd never have the chance to know those answers, never see the baby that almost was.

Her throat closed and her eyes burned. Everything would have been different if only…

"Is George all fixed now?"

Libby's voice drew Katie back again. She looked down at the reattached teddy bear head, now mostly back in place, lolling just a bit to the left. Katie choked back the lump in her throat. "He looks perfect, Libby. That's awesome. I'm so proud of what a good job you did."

"Thank you, Miss Katie." Libby beamed and leaned into Katie's side, nestling her tiny body under Katie's arm. "Thank you for helping me."

Katie hesitated a second, then wrapped her arm around Libby and drew her close. The sweet scent of strawberry shampoo wafted into the space. Libby didn't say anything, just clutched Katie's side, pressing the bear against her belly, and burrowed closer. "Thank you," she whispered again.

When she was a little girl, Katie had climbed into her mother's chair more than once and leaned into Vanessa's shoulder, seeking a hug the same as Libby was doing. Only in the cramped, musty apartments where she'd grown up, hugs had been as rare as hundred dollar bills. *You're too old for that*, her mother would say, pushing Katie down. *I'm tired and I can't deal with you kids.*

Katie might never know what kind of mother she would be with her own children, but right now, in this moment, she could be the mother she'd always wanted with these two motherless children. She could fill in those gaps as best she could, and never, ever make them feel unwanted or bothersome or unloved.

She could fix a bear and teach a girl to sew and make finger paintings and return hugs. And maybe, just maybe, doing so would begin to ease the ache in Katie's heart, too.

She drew Libby in a little closer, then pressed a gentle kiss to the girl's forehead. "You're welcome, Libby. You're very, very welcome."

Two hours later, Katie put Henry in the stroller, then took Libby's hand and set out for the fire station. Katie still had a bit of trepidation about her date with Sam afterward, and had spent way too much time fixing her hair and redoing her makeup before they'd left.

Libby carried George the entire way, holding the bear against her hip like it was a football made of gold. Henry was making small talk with an action figure he'd brought along, happy as a clam in the sun. He was a pretty happy kid overall, and talking more and more each time Katie saw him.

"Fire trucks," Henry said, reaching forward. "I see fire trucks!"

"You have to be good," Katie said. "And listen to the firemen. They're going to let you see all the trucks, and climb inside them, but only if you listen."

Libby scoffed. "He's three. He doesn't listen to anyone." Then she let out a long, dramatic sigh. The earlier moment of tenderness after the teddy bear got fixed had disappeared, and Libby was back to perfecting her annoyed eight-year-old face. "Why do we have to go see stupid fire trucks, anyway? I don't want to see any stupid trucks."

"Because Henry loves fire trucks and firemen, and my brother is going to show him the inside of the station. Besides, your dad is meeting us here."

Libby cast her gaze to the ground. "He always says that. Then he works and doesn't come."

"He'll be here," Katie said. "I'm sure of it."

Actually, she wasn't sure of any such thing. She hardly knew Sam. He could be the kind of guy who broke promises or showed up late, or never showed up at all. But he had seemed pretty adamant earlier today that he would be there, and after everything he'd said about not being involved when his kids were younger, surely he wouldn't miss this opportunity. Nor, she was sure, would he miss their date.

Katie's heart sang at the thought of seeing Sam again, and her steps seemed to lighten. She had run through her meager, hastily packed wardrobe in her mind, and realized the only dressy thing she had was a simple black dress and a pair of red pumps. Hopefully, Sam would like them. Ever since he'd stopped by this afternoon, she'd been nervously and excitedly anticipating their date.

Her gaze scanned the sidewalk, but she didn't see Sam anywhere. They reached the fire station, and Colton came out to greet them, dressed in dark blue pants and a dark blue T-shirt with the Stone Gap Fire Department logo above his heart. "I heard someone really likes fire trucks."

Henry raised his arms. "Me! Me!"

"Well, come on in, kids. I've got a lot of cool things to show you."

Katie bent down to unbuckle Henry, handing him the plastic container of cookies at the same time. "Go give those to Colton, okay?"

Henry toddled over to Colton and thrust the container up at him. "Here. I didn't eat any."

Colton laughed and took the cookies. "Maybe I'll share one later."

That made Henry smile, and he happily followed alongside Colton as the four of them went into the fire station. Libby brought up the rear, her gaze straying to the sidewalk again and again. Her face was sour, her eyes watery and her disappointment clear.

"Who wants to climb into the big engine?" Colton opened the door and helped Henry up and inside the cab. The little boy could hardly see above the dashboard, but he happily slipped into place and spun the steering wheel from side to side. Colton showed him how to honk the horn and play with the lights.

Libby hung back, her bear now in the stroller seat, while she stood listless and sad by the door. "I told you he wouldn't come," she said.

"He can still make it. We'll be here for a little while." Katie dug her phone out of her pocket and checked the text messages. Nothing from Sam. She debated contacting him, then thought maybe he'd forgotten what time they were meeting.

At the fire station with the kids. Libby is really missing you. Are you on your way?

She snapped a picture of Henry in the driver's seat of the fire engine, then sent the message off. She held the phone awhile longer, sure that there would be a quick response back. Nothing.

"See? I told you he isn't coming," Libby said. She gestured toward Katie's phone. "He probably didn't call or anything. He does that."

"I'm sure something important came up," Katie said. "Why don't you go on up in the truck with your brother? I'm sure Henry would love that."

Libby rolled her eyes, but did as Katie requested. A few other firefighters had joined Colton, and they took the kids over to the next engine parked in the bay.

Colton slipped into place beside Katie. "Thanks for the cookies."

"Thanks for doing this. I'm sure Henry's going to be over the moon for days now that he got to see inside a real fire truck."

"You know, that's how I ended up as a fireman myself. Uncle Tank took me to the fire station one day and I was hooked after that."

Uncle Tank, who both Katie and Colton had always thought was a family friend, had turned out to be Colton's natural uncle. He was the brother of Bobby Barlow, Colton's real father, and he had sort of kept tabs on Colton as he was growing up. He'd been an uncle to Katie, too, filling in for the father she'd never had.

Whoever her father had been. Vanessa had forgotten that detail in the long line of bad boyfriends she'd had. By the time Katie was old enough to ask, her mother couldn't remember which of her boyfriends had been the one to get her pregnant. Katie sometimes missed having a father, but between Colton and Uncle Tank, it had been enough. Yet at the same time, she had never given up hope that one day her father would come in, like a prince on a white horse, and whisk her into his arms and apologize for being gone so long.

Katie could understand how losing one parent could

leave a gaping hole for a child. How it had done that for Libby and Henry. Surely, Libby's mother would have known the right words to turn Libby's frown into a smile. Katie had just kept on echoing that Sam would be there, but as the minutes ticked by and the kids went from truck to truck, it became painfully clear he wasn't going to show up. Disappointment filled Katie as the excuses she'd made in her head became thinner and thinner.

"Sam's a good guy," Colton said, as if he'd read her mind. "A lot overwhelmed, but a good guy."

"His kids need him to be here," she whispered. "That's all they care about."

"He'll be there when it counts. That's the kind of man Sam Millwright is. Just give him some breathing room, let him get back on track."

Katie glanced up at Libby and Henry in the truck, Henry playing with the controls, Libby grudgingly sitting beside him. Even though it was clear Sam wasn't going to make it on time, Libby kept glancing at the door from time to time.

A little girl much like Katie had once been. A little girl who still had hope.

## Chapter Seven

Sam trudged up the front steps a little after six, exhausted, his mind awhirl with the massive to-do list still waiting on him. He had calls to make, emails to send, a brochure to write up…the list was long and daunting. And it all needed to be done yesterday. He'd run behind all day, then had a last-minute showing that took five times longer than he expected. At least those extra hours—hours he had spent touring a vacant mall space instead of being with his kids—had resulted in an offer, which meant a hefty commission to come soon. That would go a long way toward easing the financial albatross around his neck.

Except it had meant missing the kids at the fire station, and the date he and Katie were supposed to have afterward. By the time he had a chance to text Katie, they were already walking home. Apparently, he was a star student in Failing at Being a Dad 101.

Sam sighed. Every time he turned around, he was screwing things up, with the kids, with Katie. Everything had seemed to be going so well between him and Katie, with an attraction that he could no longer deny, and didn't want to. But if he kept standing her up like this, she was going to be gone before he even had a chance to see where that attraction might lead.

At least he was home now. Just as he reached for the door, his phone rang. Work, interfering again. "Hello?"

"Sam, it's Hank Osborn." The owner of the firm had a deep, booming voice, made even more so by him being on speaker. "I want to know how that mall property is coming."

"I've had several showings. I've got one fabulous offer—"

"I need all five closed by the end of the month. The anchor tenant wants to open up a month earlier, so we need the other properties settled. Signed, sealed, money in the bank. Come on, Sam, you promised you could deliver. Show me that I didn't make a mistake hiring you."

"I'm on it, Mr. Osborn," Sam said, though he wasn't sure he could pull off the miracle Hank was asking of him, and on an even tighter deadline than before. With showings booked for the weekend and two nights this week, he was already working extra hours, but somehow he was going to need to work even more. And hopefully convince Katie to watch the kids a lot more than he'd originally hired her on for. He let out a long breath. It was almost one of those be-careful-what-you-wish-for things. He had the job he needed—and he was right back to working too many hours and being home too few.

He tucked his phone away and went inside. The scents of spaghetti sauce and garlic bread greeted him, followed by the sound of the music. Some pop song, sung by a singer he couldn't name, but with a catchy beat. He put his briefcase down by the door, then headed into the kitchen.

Katie had Henry on her hip, one of his hands in hers, sashaying around the kitchen island, while Libby followed along, dancing with her bear. The three of them were singing along with the song as they danced, their faces bright and animated and happy.

Just like a family should be.

Sam stood on the periphery, watching his family have fun without him. He should have been here, should have been the one making the spaghetti and dancing with the kids. Should have been at the fire station today. Should have been home earlier. Should have upheld his promise of a date tonight. He'd missed it all—because work had been his priority again. Guilt weighed on him like a too-heavy winter coat.

He was glad Katie had made dinner. She'd probably realized the restaurant plans would have to be changed and instead of getting mad, she'd taken care of dinner. He was beyond grateful for her thoughtfulness. Now, he could stay, spend time with the kids and Katie. Maybe the day could still be salvaged, after all.

He dropped his keys on the counter, then slipped in behind the three of them. "Looks like I'm just in time for the dance party."

Libby looked back at him, then made a face, and immediately Sam felt the coolness in the air between himself and his daughter. At the same time, the song came to an end, and she stopped dancing. "You're too late. We're done now."

"It's not too late, Libby Bear. We can put on another song—"

"You're too late!" she shouted. "You're always too late!" Then she spun on her heel and ran out of the room. A second later, Sam heard the slam of Libby's bedroom door.

Katie put Henry down. "Why don't you go play with your blocks while I finish up dinner?"

Henry nodded and took off for the living room. Katie leaned over and switched off the radio, then went back to the stove. She didn't talk to him, didn't so much as acknowledge his presence.

Great. He'd ticked everybody off.

"I'm sorry I'm home so late," he began. "And I hate to do this, but I need to work Wednesday and Thursday night and both weekend days. Just a few hours, I swear. I'm hoping you can take the kids for me."

She shook her head. "I thought you told me just yesterday how you regretted working too much and not being here with your kids."

"I did. I do. But I'm just starting at a new firm and they expect a lot out of me since I'm new and I thought I'd have the flexibility I had at my old job, but there's this big mall project and..." He ran a hand through his hair. "I'm sorry, Katie."

"I'm not the one you need to apologize to." She stirred the pasta, then the sauce, and paused to check the bread sitting under the oven broiler, toasting to a golden brown. Katie tugged off her apron and laid it on the counter. She didn't look at him, didn't grace him with one of those amazing smiles. Instead, she was as distant as she would have been with a stranger. "Dinner should be ready in five more minutes. All you have to do is drain the pasta and take the bread out of the oven in a couple minutes. Everything else is done."

He glanced at the table. Three place settings had

been laid out. The fourth empty chair seemed to mock him. "You're leaving?"

"My job is done today. Enjoy your dinner."

"Wait." He reached for her and stopped her. She turned and looked at him, but her face stayed impassive and cold. The warmth and light from yesterday had dimmed. "Stay. Eat dinner with us."

"I can't." She broke away from his grip, grabbed her purse and crossed the kitchen. "I'm sorry, Sam. I'll see you tomorrow."

"Katie…"

She turned back at the doorway. Her eyes filled; her face took on a shadow. Whatever warmth had been between them the last few days was gone now. "Libby and Henry weren't the only ones disappointed today, Sam. But they're the only ones you need to make it up to. Go spend time with your kids. I'll see you tomorrow."

Later that evening, Katie was sitting on the front porch, nursing a glass of wine. After leaving Sam's house, Katie had stopped in town to do a little shopping and grab a bite to eat. When she'd gotten back to the inn, she'd sent out several emails to contacts she had in the accounting industry in Atlanta, asking about job opportunities. *Moving forward*, she told herself. Or maybe just avoiding the present. Either way, she was going to sit here and drink her wine and unwind, and not dwell on how Sam had let the kids down today.

Let her down.

"I'm heading home to my man," Della said, joining her on the porch. "Do you need anything else? Mavis is inside, and she'll have breakfast ready first thing in the morning."

Katie liked Mavis, Della's partner in the B and B.

She was a buxom African-American woman, warm and friendly, with a ready smile and a fondness for peanut butter fudge. Mavis lived on-site while Della went home to her own house a few blocks away every night. "No, I'm good. Thanks, Della."

"What happened with Sam? I thought I was supposed to watch the kids tonight while you guys went out. But he texted a while ago and said plans had changed."

"Nothing happened. We just...changed our minds." Katie took a long sip of the wine. It didn't ease her disappointment. She should be glad. After all, not dating Sam allowed her to focus on her game plan going forward. She wasn't going to be Sam's nanny forever, which meant she needed to get back to her real job. Send out some more emails tonight, make use of the contacts she had in her database. Eventually she would have to leave Stone Gap and go back to reality in Atlanta. To her apartment, her life.

Della sank into the opposite wicker chair. "You okay, honey? You look...sad."

"I just thought Sam was...different." But in the end, he did what every other man she knew did—he said a lot of fancy words about wanting to settle down and be a family man, and instead made work his family.

It all told her one thing: when she needed him, Sam wouldn't be there and she'd be left to deal with things alone. Hadn't she learned that lesson with Leonard? Seen it firsthand tonight with Sam? All those extra hours he was going to work, the trips and dinners he was going to miss?

Losing the baby had been devastating. Katie could still picture the doctor, clutching his medical chart, with this uncomfortable look of sympathy on his face. "Do you have someone to drive you home?" he'd asked.

She'd had no one to hold her hand, no one to tell her it would all be okay. She wasn't going to be stupid enough to get involved with another man who wasn't there when things got rough.

Della put a hand on Katie's. "Some men are afraid to slow down. I think they're afraid they won't be up to the challenge of kids. They can tackle a ten-hour meeting with a roomful of lawyers, or negotiate for half a day on a piece of equipment, but when it comes to kids... they get scared."

"But it's Sam's own kids. If anything, it should be easy for him." Easier, certainly, than it had been for Katie. Every time Libby or Henry hugged her or took her hand, she could sense them seeking that connection with someone maternal. Those moments still caused a little hiccup of pain in Katie's heart, a reminder that she'd blown her one and only chance at being a mother.

"I think some men feel out of their element around kids," Della went on. "All that playtime and pretending and silly song singing. And then there are all those expectations. Kids are...precious and men know that. And so many of them are afraid that if they say the wrong thing or do the wrong thing, they'll screw them up and the whole family will end up on Dr. Phil." Della smiled. "My Bobby was like that when the boys were little. He held them like they were bombs that were ready to detonate at any second. It took him a long time to relax and have fun with them. But still there were years..."

Katie waited for Della to continue, sensing that whatever she was about to say was something she didn't share often. Della toyed with the wicker arm for a long moment.

"We had some hard years when we were married," she said finally. "Bobby worked a lot, spending more time under a Buick than he did at home. And when he was there, the boys didn't know how to engage with him. They gravitated toward me, even though they loved their dad and would do anything to spend more time with him."

"What changed? Because from what Colton says, all the Barlow boys are close to their dad." Since Colton had met his biological family, he'd kept Katie updated on everything Jack, Luke, Mac and Bobby were up to. She almost felt like she knew them all, just from the conversations she'd had with her brother. She was glad he'd found a family to love, a family who clearly loved him back. And maybe she was also a teeny bit jealous, too, that he had all that. Katie would never know her real father, and had no real relationship with her mother, but she could live vicariously through Colton and maybe that would be enough.

"What changed? The flu." Della laughed softly. "I know that sounds crazy, but that's what it was. Bobby got sick first, spent three days in bed, which was unheard of for a man who worked six days a week. Then the boys got it, and then me. I could barely lift my head, I was so sick, and Bobby had to stay home and tend to the boys. At first, it was all changing sheets and making chicken soup from a can, but then the boys got better, and Bobby took them with him, fishing and to the garage, to give me time to rest. By the time I was better, the boys and Bobby were thick as thieves."

Maybe that was what Sam needed. Some one-on-one time with his kids where they were all having fun. Katie had a feeling that all Sam did when he was home alone with the kids was clean and cook and try to keep the house running. He needed to be out there, finger painting and running the hose and dancing in the kitchen.

Maybe if her own mother had done more of that, Katie would have felt like she was living with an actual parent, and not a detached roommate. "And they stayed that way ever since?"

Della nodded. "Bobby would need a little nudging from time to time, to remember what was important, but yes, he did work hard at having a relationship with his sons. And in turn, that made our marriage stronger. We were a team, in every sense of the word. And I'll tell you, when the going gets tough, that's what you need to be—a team."

Katie scoffed. "I don't think I've ever felt like that with any man."

Della got to her feet. She gave Katie's shoulder a pat. "Those kind of men are out there. They're rare, but that's what makes them so special."

She twirled the wineglass, watching the liquid rise and fall against the curved edge. "I don't know where I'm going to find one."

A smile curved across Della's face. "There are an awful lot of men like that right here in Stone Gap. You might have already met one." Then she said good-night and headed down the stairs and out to her car.

Katie sipped the rest of her wine and watched the lights of Stone Gap turn on and off. People going home, having dinner, reading bedtime stories, saying goodnight. The night was warm, the air carrying the faint scent of ocean, and the streets were quiet, punctuated by the occasional call of a night bird. Katie started to get to her feet when she saw a set of headlights coming down the street, then stopping outside the Stone Gap Inn.

Sam stepped out of his car and stood in the pale white glow of the streetlight. Katie's heart stuttered.

"Can we talk?" he said.

"Where are the kids?"

"After they were asleep, I asked Colton to come by. I figured if Henry woke up, he'd be in heaven, with a real-life firefighter in his house." Sam gestured toward the porch. "Can I come up there?"

If he sat beside her, she'd be tempted to touch him, to lean into him, despite everything that had happened this afternoon. "Do you want anything to drink?"

"A beer would be fabulous."

"I'll go grab one." She welcomed the opportunity to go in the house, to take a few seconds to grab a beer for Sam and on the way back, primp in the mirror. Not that she cared what he thought, of course. But that didn't stop her from smoothing a few flyaway strands of hair or checking to make sure her eye makeup hadn't smudged. She went outside to the porch and handed Sam his drink. "Here you go."

"Thanks." He took the beer in both palms, but didn't drink. "I'm sorry about today. And tonight."

"It's okay. I told you."

"No, it's not okay. You're right. But I just can't seem to find a way to make it all work. My new job is more demanding than I had expected, and that means I need to put in the hours, make the connections, send out the emails. But I can't do that and be home and be present, too. There are only so many hours in the day."

"Then you have to prioritize." She sat back in the wicker chair, easing into the thick cushion. "Your kids need you, Sam. They want to have a relationship with you. I'm just the nanny and I won't be there forever. But you will be."

She'd taken steps tonight to make her return to Atlanta. She'd thought it would make her sleep easier, but instead, the thought of going back there made her...sad.

He sighed. "There's so much to worry about, so many things to remember, to do."

"You don't have to do everything, Sam. Just the things that are important."

"It's all important, Katie. Making sure the kids have a roof over their heads, food in their bellies, shoes to wear to school—those are my first priorities. Those have to come before watching Henry climb on a fire truck."

She thought of what Della had said, and about what she herself had seen in Sam over the last couple weeks. How he escaped instead of being plugged in. With his kids, with her. He'd missed more than just a fire truck adventure tonight, and she had to wonder if she was lumped in there in his mind with all the other things that he had to do. "Are you sure you aren't just using work as an excuse?"

"What kind of excuse could I be looking for?"

"Maybe..." She fiddled with the stem of the wine-glass. "Maybe you're afraid that you lost that connection to the kids and you're working so you don't have to deal with that. Or find out that it's too late to restore it."

He got to his feet. "You don't have children, Katie. You don't know how tough this is. You know what I'm most afraid of? Letting my kids down. Losing the only things they have left—the house, the toys, the things that remind them of their mother. So I go to work every day and pay the bills and pray that I don't end up in a car accident, too, and leave my kids with no one."

The words hit her hard. She scrambled to her feet and took several steps away. "Just because I don't have kids doesn't mean I don't understand or that I can't sympathize with you."

"I... I don't mean to say that. It's just different when

you finally hold your child. There's this feeling that comes over you, and it's so powerful and so overwhelming. In that moment, when you look down at your baby's face, you know there is nothing in the world that could ever be more important than that child."

Her hand went to her belly, to the space that had once held her own baby. From the minute she'd realized she was pregnant, she'd felt that sense of protection. But in the end, her body had betrayed her, and the baby she'd sworn to keep safe had died, without ever seeing the world. Then she thought of her mother. Had there ever been a moment when Vanessa had looked at Katie and felt that kind of overpowering love and protection? Or had she seen only the work, the responsibilities involved?

"Maybe someday I'll know what that's like," Katie said softly.

He laid a hand on her shoulder. "When that day comes, I'm sure you'll be a great mom, Katie."

She shook her head and cursed the tears that burned the back of her eyes. "You don't know that."

"I've seen you with my kids. They love you, and are doing so well with you. And I know you're right. I should be there more." Sam sat still for a long time, not saying a word. His gaze dropped to the floor, and he dangled the beer between his fingers. "What if…"

"What?" she prompted, when he didn't finish.

"What if I suck at being with them? What if I can't do the crafts or remember Libby's favorite cereal or tuck Henry in with the right bedtime story? What if I'm not—" he lifted his gaze now, and she saw a shimmer in his eyes "—as good of a parent as my wife was?"

"You won't be the same parent your wife was, no matter what you do, Sam." She drew in a breath. "You're you, and that's awesome just the way you are. I see the way they light up when you are around."

"Henry, yes, but Libby…" He shook his head. "When I was a kid, my dad worked all the time. I vowed I would be a different father, that I would be there to build the tree houses and play the games and read the stories. Then we brought Libby home from the hospital and she cried for, I swear, six months straight. Wendy was the only one who could soothe her, get her to eat, sleep. I felt…left out. So I worked and worked, and by the time Henry came along, my career was in full swing and it just—" he let out a breath " became easier to work instead of…"

"Failing again," she finished. She knew that avoidance technique. Heck, she could have written the book on it. "You're not the only one who uses work to avoid the hard stuff, Sam. When I was young, it was school. I was OCD student of the year. I kept thinking if I got better grades, my parents would show up in my life. They never did. Later, I replaced that with work. It was a…"

"Refuge," Sam finished for her.

She nodded. "Exactly."

He ticktocked the beer back and forth. "We're so much alike, Katie. It's no wonder I'm attracted to you."

Just like that, the tone between them shifted. She could feel the wine kicking in, making her a little warmer, a little braver. "You're attracted to me?"

He got to his feet, then reached out and crossed to her. "I think that's been pretty obvious from the beginning."

"Hot for teacher, huh?" She gave him a flirty smile.

"Hot for a teacher who makes a simple skirt look like a sin." He smiled back, then closed the gap between them and kissed her. Like their first kiss, it was sweet and tender, slow and easy.

Or at least it started that way. As soon as Katie leaned into him, Sam's body responded. He clutched her tighter and kissed her deeper. She curved her small frame into him, yet she fit exactly against his chest. His hands roamed over her back, her buttocks, her hips, then back up again, wanting more, yet at the same time painfully aware that they were standing on Della's front porch, and a kiss was as far as they could go.

With reluctance, he stepped back. But he didn't let go. His hands cupped her cheeks, his brown eyes locking on hers. Heat filled the space between them. "Tomorrow, I swear I will work a half day. Libby has a half day at school, Henry will be back early from the community center. As soon as the kids are home, let's take them to the beach."

"Both of us? But you don't need me there. You'll be fine with the kids."

"I don't *need* you there. I *want* you there. Will you go?"

Her eyes were wide and shiny in the dim light from the porch. She hesitated only a second, then nodded. "You had me at beach day."

He laughed. God, it felt good to laugh. To smile. To flirt. "Then I'm going to have to say that more often. Much, much more often."

## Chapter Eight

Bandit darted in and out of the water, barking at the small waves that rolled onto the sandy shore. Libby waded in up to her ankles, while Henry, the more adventurous one, sat in the surf and let the water wash up to his waist while he tried to build a sand castle in between waves. The remains of the kids' sandwiches—a result of a quick pit stop at the Good Eatin' Café on the way over to the beach—lay atop paper plates on a checkered blanket.

It was a perfect way to spend the afternoon. Absolutely perfect.

That didn't mean that Sam wasn't thinking about work, though, or worrying that the appointment he had rescheduled, the emails he hadn't had a chance to send, and the calls that were going to his voice mail, were going to cost him down the road. The mall project wasn't going to rent itself.

But then Sam thought about the surprise on his kids'

faces when he'd walked into the house, and the whoop of joy Libby had let out when he'd said they were going to the beach. That alone was worth him working late tonight or getting up super-early tomorrow to finish up. For now, there was the beach, the sandwiches, the kids and Katie.

Sam leaned back on one elbow and stretched his legs. The sun warmed his skin, danced sparkles on the sand. "Thank you again for reminding me to take time off," he said to Katie. "This is...awesome. I feel like I don't spend hardly any time outside anymore."

"Me, too. I spent way too much time indoors at my job." She leaned back on both elbows beside him and tipped her face to the sun. Her dark hair hung like a curtain down her back, and there was a look of pure contentment on her face. He could just catch the faint scent of her perfume stirring in the air between them. Something dark, floral. Tempting. "This is nice."

"Very nice."

He'd stopped noticing the weather and the ocean because all he saw was Katie. She was beautiful, graceful. He took in the long curve of her neck and the gentle ridges of her shoulders, the delicate lines of her arms. She was wearing khaki shorts and a dark blue V-necked T-shirt. Specks of red paint from this afternoon's art project with Henry dotted her clothes, freckled her arms, and only enticed Sam more.

He wanted to ask her a thousand questions, wanted to know what made her smile, whether she was a chocolate or vanilla ice cream kind of girl, what movies made her laugh, which books made her cry.

Sam cleared his throat and returned his attention to the kids instead of staring at the woman he'd hired to be the nanny. That blanket of guilt still hung on his shoulders. He barely had enough time to be more than a token dad to his kids—what was he doing pursuing the woman working for him? If anything had cliché written all over it, it was the idea of falling for the nanny.

Libby came running up the beach, Bandit and Henry hot on her heels. Still wet from the surf, Henry's shorts dripped onto the sand, while Bandit panted beside him, tail wagging. "I'm bored," Libby said.

The most common words ever spoken by kids, Sam thought. How many times had he heard that from Libby? Heck, how often had he said it himself when he was a kid?

His father's solution—if his father had been there at all—would have been to send his two boys out back and tell them to find something to do. Their mother, often overwhelmed by raising two rambunctious boys, would opt to lie down for a nap or get lost in a soap opera, leaving Sam and Dylan to fend for themselves. He refused to let his kids grow up that way.

"Why don't we build a sand castle?" Sam said.

"I'm too old for that. That's what babies do and I'm not a baby anymore." She crossed her arms over her chest and pouted. "I wanna go home."

They'd been here only a half hour. If they went home, the kids would beeline for the TV, Sam would opt for his computer and this sweet moment in the sun would end. But when he tried to think of things that Libby might want to do, he drew a blank. When had it gotten this way? When had he lost track of his kids and what made them happy?

He knew that answer. When his wife had died and taken with her the gentle reminders to put down his work and engage with his kids, along with all that inside knowledge of a woman who had spent every spare second with her kids. Somehow, he needed to navigate these murky waters without Wendy.

"We could take a walk," Sam said.

Libby rolled her eyes. "I don't wanna do that with you. I wanna go home."

*I don't wanna do that with you.* The words pierced his heart. Sam could see Libby digging in her heels, and braced himself for the battle that was about to storm in. Henry lingered behind his sister, eyes downcast, face somber. Even Bandit had plopped down on the sand, his tail still, ears drooping.

There'd been a day when Libby would have rushed into his arms whenever he got home from work. When she had called out "Daddy!" like she'd just won the lottery. When she would have walked for hours with him, chattering on about her day or her toys or the little girl who lived next door. Now, Libby looked like she'd rather be anywhere but here with him.

He had only himself to blame. Those years of working too late, getting home after the kids were in bed, putting in extra hours on the weekend, or "spending time" with the kids while he was on his laptop and not really doing much more in common than breathing the same air, had taken their toll. There was no Wendy here to remind him to put down the keyboard or to take an hour off. There was just him, trying to balance everything without losing it all in the process. Judging by the look on Libby's face, he wasn't doing very well at either.

He might as well cave now to Libby's request and stave off the foot stomping and tears. If she didn't want to be here, the whole day would end up a bust, and that wasn't going to help anything. "Okay." He let out a breath. "Let me just get all this stuff packed up."

"Before you do that, I have an idea," Katie said, laying a hand on his for a second, saying *trust me* in that touch, before she turned her attention to Libby. "When I was a kid, and I got bored, my brother would take me on what he called adventure trips."

"What's an adventure trip?" Libby asked. She still wore that sullen look, but her eyes had brightened with interest. Sam shifted toward Katie, just as intrigued. Her idea already sounded a heck of a lot better than the two options he'd proposed.

"We didn't have a beach in Atlanta," Katie explained, "so we'd go down to a creek in our neighborhood or into the woods behind my school, and we'd look for animals and weird objects. Whoever found the coolest animal or the weirdest thing won a prize."

"A prize?" That had piqued her interest even more. "What kind of prize?"

"Well…" Katie glanced over at Sam, saying *fill in the blanks*.

He thought of what would make Libby the most excited, what kind of prize would entice her to play the game instead of insisting on going home. "How about first dibs on what movie we watch before bed tonight?"

"Even if it's *Frozen*?" Libby narrowed her gaze and propped a fist on her hip.

Sam bit back a groan. He had seen Libby's all-time favorite movie twelve trillion times already and usually vetoed it at bedtime because there was only so many times a grown man could listen to "Let It Go." But it was the one thing guaranteed to bring a smile to Libby's face, so that meant he'd listen to Elsa all night if he needed to. "Even if it's *Frozen*."

Libby turned back to Katie. She bounced on her heels. "Okay, I wanna do an adventure. What do we have to find?"

Katie got to her feet and brushed the sand off her palms. "It's the most fun when you have teams. So... how about me and Henry go against your dad and you, Libby?"

Libby sobered and looked up at Katie. "But I wanna be with you, Katie."

She caught Sam's gaze over Libby's head. He nodded, saying *let it go.* If he pushed Libby too hard and too fast, it would only make things worse.

"Okay, Libby," Katie said, "but I think we're going to have our work cut out for us." Sam hoisted Henry onto his hip and ruffled Libby's hair. Henry looked from his sister to his father, then rested his head on Sam's shoulder.

"Don't count on it," Sam said. "Us boys are serious competitors."

"Want to put a wager on it?" Katie asked him.

When she looked at him like that, with that little bit of a tease in her eyes, he'd agree to pretty much anything. "What kind of wager?"

"Winning team—" she thought for a second, a finger against her lip "—buys dessert on the way home."

"You're on." He put out a hand. When she slipped her palm into his, a little jolt ran up his arm. She had small, delicate fingers, but a firm grip. He didn't want to let go, but didn't think standing here and holding the nanny's hand was going to do anything other than confuse everyone. Especially him. Not that those kisses hadn't already muddled everything, anyway. He kept wavering between wanting to take her to bed and staying hands-off. Since he didn't have an answer to any of those dilemmas, he got back to the game. "Okay, where do we start?"

"With the little stuff, Sam." Her eyes met his, and

in them he could read understanding, compassion. She had seen his struggle with Libby and stepped in, with this simple game. That made him like Katie on a whole new level. "The big stuff will follow."

Katie didn't know what it was about Sam, but every time she looked at him, she wanted to melt. It wasn't just that he was handsome as heck, or that he had that sweet lopsided smile. It was the way he tried so hard to connect with his kids. She could see his heart breaking every time Libby gave him the cold shoulder or Henry refused to talk, and she wanted to do whatever she could to make that all better.

She'd lingered after lunch because she enjoyed spending time with Sam, with the kids. She'd have stayed even if she wasn't getting paid. She enjoyed the kids, and most of all, enjoyed seeing Sam smile.

Then she'd proposed the adventure game, the same one Colton had played with her. Only, when she was little, he hadn't taken her on adventures to stave off boredom or get her out of the house when their mother was in a bad mood. He'd done it to distract her from yet another disappointment. Another day in a house with a distant parent.

They had broken into two teams, with Sam and Henry running up ahead of Katie and Libby. Their goal: to find an intact clamshell. She'd given Henry and Libby each one of the plastic bags that had held their lunch, and told them there were extra points for finding the most interesting piece of trash.

"Look, Katie!" Libby held out her palm and revealed a sandy plastic army man, a little worse for wear. "I found this!"

"That's pretty cool," Katie said. "When I was a little

girl, my brother had army men like this. I took them and buried them in the backyard."

Libby gasped. "Did you get in big trouble with your mommy?"

Big trouble? Her mother had barely noticed Katie was home, never mind anything she did. "My mom worked a lot," Katie said. "So she didn't really know. But Colton, oh, he was mad at me for about a day. Longest day of my life." She laughed. "I love my brother, even if he sometimes drives me crazy."

"Kinda like how I feel about Henry. He's kinda cute but he cries a lot." Libby turned the army man over in her palm. "And he plays with my Barbies. I don't want him to 'cuz he eats their hair."

Katie laughed. "When he gets older, he won't do that anymore. And you never know, you two might even become friends."

Libby's nose wrinkled. "I don't think so."

"Give it time." Ahead of them, Sam was bent down, looking at something Henry had found, their two heads close together. Such a heartwarming image, with the sun glinting off their dark hair and twin smiles on their faces. For a second, Katie stopped walking and just stared.

There was something inherently sexy about a man who connected with children. Who could get down to their level. Sam was exclaiming over whatever Henry had in his hand, making as big a deal out of it as he would about finding a unicorn. Henry was smiling, clearly proud of himself.

She wondered for a second how things might have been different if she'd been dating Sam and gotten pregnant. Would Sam have left? Or would he have stayed by her side, every step of the way? Even in those dark days after she lost the baby?

"Katie, are we gonna find a clamshell? 'Cuz I really want to beat the boys."

"Uh, sure, sure." Katie turned her attention back to Libby and concentrated on scouring the beach.

A few minutes later, Sam ambled over, with Henry following right beside him. "Looks like somebody's buying me a slice of coconut cream pie," Sam said, then splayed his palm to reveal a complete clamshell, still hinged on one side.

"I don't know about that. I think someone's getting me a slice of chocolate cake." Katie held out the army man Libby had found. "Best trash piece."

"Hmm…looks like a tie." Sam grinned. "And what do we do in that case, oh adventure master?"

"We treat everyone to dessert," she said, thinking if he kept on smiling at her like that, she'd pay for dessert, dinner and breakfast the next morning. Damn, this man had so much power over her with something as simple as a smile.

"Ice cream?" Libby asked. "'Cuz I love ice cream!"

"I—scream," Henry echoed.

Sam glanced down at his son, his face lit with wonder, and his smile widened when he leaned closer to whisper in Katie's ear. "I'm never going to get tired of the sound of his voice. Thank you again."

She inhaled his cologne, and tried not to let her gaze linger on the dark stubble along his jaw. "I didn't do anything."

"You opened a door that had been shut," he said softly. "And for that, I should be buying *you* dessert. And much more."

She wanted to ask what he meant by much more, but

Libby was tugging at her arm and charging back up the beach toward the car. Probably just as well. She wasn't staying here and wasn't going to become mom to these kids. All of this was temporary.

A few minutes later, they were all settled in Sam's Range Rover and heading toward downtown Stone Gap. She could see why Colton enjoyed this town so much. It was quaint, with pastel homes flanking tree-lined streets, small wrought-iron benches peppered between old-fashioned streetlights. Every couple blocks there was a green space, either a park or a giant water fountain or just a trio of benches, encouraging people to sit and talk awhile. And everywhere she looked, there were people, walking between stores or sitting together and sipping coffee, or tossing a ball for their spaniel to fetch.

"Is it always like this here?" She glanced over at Sam.

"What, boring?"

She laughed. "I think Stone Gap is the opposite of boring. It's just so…quaint."

"It is a great town. I've lived here all my life and as much as I complain about how things stay the same year after year, I love it here. I couldn't imagine living anywhere else." His gaze flicked to the rearview mirror's reverse image of the kids, belted into the backseat. "Or raising my kids anywhere else."

Even if Sam had gotten a little disconnected over the years, Katie could see he was clearly a man who put his family first. Her mind wandered again to the questions she'd had earlier. Would things have been different if she'd been with Sam instead of Leonard? She shook her head. It didn't matter. Thinking of what could have been never led anywhere productive. "It does look like a great family town," she said.

"Pretty much everyone who was raised here stays here. Every day is like a high school reunion." He chuckled. "Which means everyone knows everything about everyone else. There truly are no secrets in a small town."

"But there's also connections, like you said," Katie added, as they passed a group of women greeting each other with hugs. "I think that's nice. Always knowing your neighbors, seeing friends you've known for years in the grocery store. Where I grew up, it wasn't like that."

"Because Atlanta's a big city?"

"Because my mom was always moving us. She didn't make much money, and every year or two we'd have to find a new apartment. Which meant a new school for me, a new neighborhood. Nothing ever stayed the same." She danced her fingers across the window as they passed two families standing on the sidewalk, chatting, twin strollers between them. "I always wondered what it would be like to live someplace like this. I can see why Colton loves it."

"He's a good guy," Sam said. "Really helped this town out after Ernie's hardware store burned down. Colton and his brothers were there the next day, rebuilding it all so quick, Ernie barely lost a dollar of business."

It made her proud to hear someone else say such good things about her brother. "He's always been like that. Best big brother a girl could ask for."

"I have a younger brother myself," Sam said. "He was the one who got in so much trouble that by the time my parents got to me, they were plumb worn out. I hardly ever got grounded. But Dylan, well, let's just say there was a reason I made a sign for the door to his room that said Detention Center."

Katie laughed. "That's terrible. What did he do when he saw the sign?"

"He loved it. When my mom was at the store one day, Dylan painted black stripes on his door. Really going for the whole in-jail feel, he said. That stunt got him another week of being grounded."

"Did your parents make him clean off the paint?"

"My mother, like yours, was pretty uninvolved and my dad was always working, so the paint stayed. My father said if Dylan wanted to pretend his room was a prison, he could. Dylan left home a few years later, in his late teens." Sam's face softened. "Haven't seen my brother in a long, long time. Or my parents. I see them maybe once or twice a year."

"I understand that." She was already having trouble imagining the years ahead, with Colton living several hours away. They'd always been close, even after Colton had moved out when he was nineteen. He'd always been there, just a text or phone call away. Even though she didn't need him now like she had when she was little and her mother forgot to pick her up at school, there was a certain comfort in knowing he always had her back.

"Are we there yet?" Libby's voice came in a long, drawn-out whine from the backseat. "Henry is kicking me and I want ice cream and I have to pee."

Sam chuckled. "Just got here, Libby Bear. Remember how we used to go here every Tuesday? We'd get ice cream for dinner, and then everyone's bellies would be sore." He turned right, then parked the car and shut it off. "Now, wait—"

But Libby had already unbuckled her seat belt and was making a beeline for the shop. Sam called out to her, but she didn't slow, heading straight inside the busy ice cream store. Sam grabbed her bear and sighed. "I swear, there are times I'm talking to myself."

Katie could see his frustration. Despite the moment of détente at the beach today, Libby was still distancing herself from her father. "I'll get her."

"Thank you. I'll be in right behind you." He leaned over to unbuckle Henry while Katie headed inside. She weaved her way through the crush of people waiting to order ice cream. No little brunette girl anywhere.

Panic raced through her. "Libby?"

The salesgirl at the counter glanced up at Katie. "Looking for a little one, about eight years old?"

Katie scanned the small shop again. "Did she come in here?"

The girl handed an elderly woman a vanilla cone, then nodded in the other direction. "Bathroom, down the hall, on the right."

"Thank you." Relief washed over Katie and she headed toward the restrooms. The bathroom was small, just two stalls, and painted a bright pink with white trim. The sink was shaped like a chocolate dipped waffle cone, and there was an ice cream cone stool in one corner. Even the soap dispenser was shaped like a sundae, and probably dispensed vanilla scented soap. One of the stall doors was closed, but Katie could see a familiar pair of pink flip-flops.

"Hey, Libby? You should have waited for us," Katie said. "We didn't know where you went."

From the other side of the closed stall door came a sniffle and a muffled, "I don't care."

Was Libby crying? Why? "Uh, are you almost done?" Katie asked. "I bet your dad and brother are waiting in line for us."

Another sniffle, another mumbled, "I don't care."

Katie stood in the bathroom, hesitating. Should she leave Libby alone? Did a girl that age need help washing her hands or anything? Was she sniffling because she was upset or mad or throwing a tantrum? And what was Katie supposed to do about any of those? Maybe she should get Sam. Except this was the ladies' room, and not the best place for a dad to talk to his daughter. "Uh, Libby, I'm just going to wait with your dad, unless you need something…"

No answer. Just more sniffling, and then the soft sound of crying. That was definitely not a tantrum. Katie's heart broke. Oh, how she understood those tears, that feeling of not being understood and just wanting to escape.

Katie went to the pink metal door and laid a hand on the cool surface. "Libby? You okay?"

"Just leave me alone."

Katie considered doing just that. She wasn't a mom, she didn't know anything about raising kids, and this crying thing seemed like something Sam should handle. The soft sounds of Libby's sobs and heaving breaths tugged at Katie.

She thought of that first summer she'd gone to camp—long before the summer she was a camp counselor. She'd been seven and terrified from the minute her mother's car pulled away, because it was also the first time she'd been somewhere without Colton in the next room.

Scared and lonely, Katie had run and hid in the bathroom. She'd huddled in the corner stall until after lights out. One of the counselors, a college student named Michelle, had found Katie in the bathroom. Michelle had sat on the floor outside the stall door and talked to her for a long, long time, until Katie's tears dried up and she'd unlatched the door. Michelle wasn't old enough to know how to be a mother, but she'd done the one thing Katie could do for Libby—she'd talked and listened and simply been there.

Katie slid down against the corner of the stall and sat on the tiles. She drew her knees up to her chest and pressed her back against the cold hard metal panel. "I'll just wait here for you, Libby. Okay?"

"You don't have to. I'm a big girl."

"I know that. But I'm gonna wait, anyway." Katie brushed at some dirt on her knees and tried to think of something to talk about that would distract Libby and calm her down. "Did you know that one cow makes enough milk to make two gallons of ice cream every day? That's a lot of milk."

Libby didn't say anything, just sniffled some more. Cried a little more.

Katie had already exhausted her list of interesting ice cream facts. "So what's your favorite flavor of ice cream, Libby? I bet it's…strawberry. Am I right?"

"That was… Mommy's favorite." Libby's voice had gone soft and sad, with a little sob on the end of "Mommy."

Oh, damn. Why had Katie brought that up? Now Libby really was crying, and it was all Katie's fault. Libby was miserable and locked inside the bathroom stall, instead of out in the shop with her father and brother. Clearly, Katie sucked at this mothering thing. Heck, she wasn't even very good at the being-a-friend-to-a-kid thing.

Katie's cell buzzed with a text from Sam. Where are you two?

Libby's a little upset. Talking to her in the bathroom. Out in a few minutes.

She hoped. Katie spun on the tile floor and rapped at the base of the stall door. She could see two little feet in pink flip-flops, swinging back and forth against the cream ceramic floor. "Libby? Why don't you come out? Your dad and brother are waiting for us to get some ice cream."

"No." It was a muffled word, still caught in a sob. Heartbroken. Lonely. Scared.

"I bet it's hard being here without your mom," Katie said softly. Silence on the other side of the door was underwritten by the Muzak sound system. "Did she like ice cream a lot?"

"Uh-huh."

"And you said her favorite was strawberry?" Katie wasn't so sure asking Libby about her dead mother was the best way to get her to come out from behind that bathroom door, but when she was seven and scared at camp and Michelle was on the other side of the stall door, Katie had talked about the things that scared her and the things that made her sad, and after a while, that feeling of being overwhelmed began to abate, and the room that had felt so stark and cold began to feel... warm. Maybe the same would work with Libby.

She hoped.

"My mom's favorite was chocolate," Katie went on, filling the space between them with words. "But I only remember going out for ice cream once with her."

"Only one time? How come?"

"My mom...wasn't home a lot," Katie said, couching the truth. "So my big brother took me for ice cream. Every Wednesday, we went after school. I always got a two-scoop cone. Chocolate on the bottom, vanilla on top, but he was more of a purist and got just one scoop of chocolate. So, what's your favorite, Libby?"

There was a long pause. The Muzak switched to an instrumental version of the Bee Gees' "Staying Alive." Another text from Sam, with another reassurance sent back from Katie. In the texts, she sounded a lot more confident that she had this under control than she felt.

"I like vanilla," Libby said after a long while. "And sprinkles. Do you like sprinkles?"

"I do. They're the best part of an ice cream cone."

"My mommy liked sprinkles, too. But she called them…um, jim…jim something."

"Jimmies," Katie supplied.

"Yeah, jimmies." The pink flip-flops toed a circle on the floor. "She said that's what they were called where she grew up."

Katie could hear the sadness in the little girl's voice, the wistful melancholy at the memories of her late mother. It made Katie want to reach her arms through the door and hug Libby, and tell her it would be all right. But she couldn't do that, and especially couldn't promise that. "What do you say we both get an ice cream with sprinkles on it? I bet that would make your mom smile."

"But…my mom can't see me," Libby said, her voice low and sad again.

"I think maybe she can," Katie said. "When I was about your age, Libby, my grandma got sick. I loved my grandma, and was really upset that I was going to lose her. I remember she was sitting in her favorite chair by the window. It was a great big chair, with pink floral fabric, but it was just the right size for her and me to sit together. She had me climb up beside her, and when I did, she pointed out the window, at the bright blue sky, and said to me, 'Do you see that space, the one just past that little cloud? That's where I'm going to be, watching over you.'"

Libby sniffled again, then asked, "Can you see her there?"

"I wish I could, but the clouds are just so far away that I can't. But I know she's there, and sometimes, I just send a little wave toward the sky, to tell her I miss her." Katie had done that dozens of times when she was younger, missing the grandmother who had been more of a mother than her own mother. Grandma Martha had been the one to bake cookies, decorate for Christmas and hang the pictures Katie colored on the fridge. Then she had died and Colton had stepped in to be the parent they were both lacking. "I've always liked knowing that she was up there, watching over me."

A long, long pause, then finally, there was a shuffling on the other side of the door, followed by the click of the lock sliding out of its home. Libby poked her head around the corner of the door frame. "Do you think my mommy could see me if I wave toward her?"

Libby's eyes shimmered with unshed tears, and her lower lip trembled. Katie's heart broke a little. "Yes, honey, I'm sure she can."

"After…" Libby drew in a breath, steeled herself a little. "After we get an ice cream with jimmies, can we go outside, so my mommy can see my ice cream, and I can say hi?"

"I think that's a wonderful idea. We can do that, for sure."

A tentative smile wobbled on Libby's face, before she dropped her gaze to the floor and gave a little nod. "Okay."

There was a knock at the bathroom door, then Sam poked his head in. "You girls okay in here?"

"We are now," Katie said. She gave Libby another smile, and this time Libby's smile held. Katie got to her feet, waited while they both washed their hands, then Libby put her palm into Katie's. The two of them crossed the room and fell into place beside Sam. "I think we're ready for some ice cream right now."

"With jimmies," Libby added softly.

"With jimmies," Katie promised, and gave Libby's hand a tender squeeze.

## Chapter Nine

Sam wanted to ask Katie what had happened back in the bathroom, but didn't want to upset the delicate balance that had been restored to Libby. She no longer seemed angry or upset, but more…peaceful. She stood beside Katie, holding her hand, and as they shuffled forward in line, Libby leaned against Sam's arm. Henry had fallen asleep, his thirty pounds of body weight a solid chunk against Sam's chest. It was as close to a perfect moment as Sam had felt in a long time.

He glanced over at Katie. She was reading the long list of ice cream flavors chalked on the slate board behind the counter. For the tenth time, he marveled at how this woman—a complete stranger—had brought a little calm into the chaos that had been his life for the last year and a half.

Libby said something about cows and milk, but Sam didn't hear the words, because whatever Libby said

made Katie smile. The curve of her lips, the way her reaction lit her eyes, captivated Sam. It was a warm smile,
the kind that spread through him like a warm fire.

In the year and a half since Wendy had died, Sam
had barely noticed other women. He hadn't dated, hell,
hadn't had time to do the laundry, never mind date,
but also hadn't had the desire to ask another woman
out. He'd loved Wendy, loved her from the first day
he'd met her when they'd been paired up in chemistry
class and she'd added too much baking soda to their
faux volcano and created a Vesuvius-worthy reaction.
After she died, he'd never imagined he'd meet another
woman who would intrigue him as much as his late
wife had. Until now.

Guilty feelings still clung to the edges of his
thoughts, but they were a little quieter. Maybe it was
time to move on, to open his heart again.

Katie turned, and caught him staring. A faint blush
filled her cheeks. "What? Do I have sand on my face
or something?"

"No, not at all." He wanted to say something more
about how beautiful she was, but figured doing that
while waiting in line for an ice cream with his kids
wasn't the best timing. "Uh, what flavor are you getting?"

"I'm going with the tried-and-true," Katie said. "A
two-scoop cone, chocolate on the bottom and—"

"Vanilla on the top," Libby added. "I wanna try that,
too."

"Sounds like a great idea," Sam said. "How about
we make it three?" Five minutes later, the three of them
had identical cones, all topped with sprinkles, and a
small dish of vanilla for Henry. Sam weaved his way
through the crowd and led them to the outside picnic

tables. Just before they sat down, Libby looked at Katie, then the two of them raised their cones to the sky. They held that position for a second, Libby's eyes glistening.

Henry woke up, and scrambled down to get his ice cream dish from Sam. The two kids opted to sit at a small table a few feet away, while Sam and Katie chose a nearby bench. "What was that about?" Sam asked.

"Libby was missing her mom, so I told her that her mom was watching her from up above, and she'd want to see that Libby was getting their favorite ice cream today."

The thoughtfulness and the heartfelt meaning in that moment made Sam choke up a little. He glanced over at his little girl, and saw her smiling, laughing, engaged with Henry. She had her bear propped up on the seat beside her as she ate her ice cream, and from time to time she would glance up at the sky. A wistful smile ghosted on Libby's face, then she turned back to her brother, her mood lighter, the tension in her tiny frame eased.

"That's…really sweet," Sam said. "Thank you."

Katie shrugged. "It was nothing."

"No, really, it was great. Libby's been struggling so much. Heck, both kids have. I wish I had the right words to help them, and it seems all I do is make it worse." He was too busy making sure everyone ate dinner and got to school and went to bed on time, and knew he was missing these small moments. The kind of moments that mattered in the long journey of healing broken hearts. "Maybe I should get them into counseling or something."

"I'm no expert," Katie said, "but I think all they need is more of what they had today."

His gaze lingered on his kids, his heart full, his throat thick. Henry struggled to scoop up the next bite, his little face scrunched with frustration. Libby leaned over, wriggled the spoon into the ice cream, then held it out to her little brother. Sam knew there would be squabbles in the days ahead—heck, maybe even in the next five minutes—but he let this moment linger.

"I'm trying, Katie, but it's been tough. Especially with Libby." He sighed. "Libby wanted to leave almost the second she got to the beach. *You* were the one who convinced her to stay and play that game. *You* were the one who talked to her in the bathroom. *You* were the one who thought of how she could share her ice cream with her mother. I think I lost whatever relationship I had with her."

"Maybe. Or maybe—" Katie paused "—you need to treat parenting like buildings."

He chuckled and took a bite of his ice cream. "You're comparing raising kids to real estate?"

"Well, when you look at a building, you get this gut instinct, I'm sure, of what it could be in the future. You know which clients to call, how to advertise the property, how to make the qualities stand out and how to minimize the flaws."

"And how does that compare to raising kids?"

"Well, you try to put a positive spin on the stuff the kids don't want to do, like eat broccoli, and try to anticipate their needs and wants." She took a few bites of her ice cream, before it melted over the edge of the cone. "It's how I worked with clients at the accounting firm. Stands to reason that if it worked with high-maintenance adults, it should work with kids."

He laughed. "Very true."

Henry and Libby squabbled a little over space on the curved bench seat at the table, the argument settled by Libby putting George on her lap. "Maybe I worry too much," Sam said. "These kids have been through so much. The last thing I want to do is make a single second of their lives more difficult."

"I think you're doing great." Katie finished her ice cream and tossed the napkin in the trash, then returned to sit beside Sam. The kids finished their treats and asked if they could play on the swing set in the small grassy area beside the ice cream shop.

"For ten minutes," Sam said. "Then it's time to go home."

Libby made a face, but didn't argue. She left her bear on the bench with Katie and Sam, then spun on her heel and chased after Henry, both of them dashing up the slide. Libby took Henry's hand at the top and let him go first. For all her complaining about her brother, Sam could see this protective side in Libby that told him she secretly did love Henry. It was nice, and told him maybe—just maybe—he was doing a few things right.

"So what about you?" he asked Katie as they walked the perimeter of the small park. Sam had the stuffed bear tucked under his arm. "How is it that an incredible woman like you is still single? I'd expect you to be married and raising a couple kids of your own."

She paused a long time. So long, he almost asked the question again. "I guess the right opportunity hasn't come along," she finally said.

"Opportunity? You make it sound like a job search." He chuckled. "Marriage is great, you know. I really did enjoy being married. And having kids, as tough as it can be some days, is wonderful. I'd love to get married again, maybe even have more kids. If the right opportunity comes along." He winked at her, expecting her to laugh.

Instead a shadow passed over her face, and the light

mood from earlier evaporated. Her body seemed to tense, and her steps slowed. "I think the ten minutes are up. We should probably get going so you can get the kids home."

But if he did that, the day with Katie would end, and suddenly, Sam didn't want to say goodbye. "Why don't I call Della and have her come over after the kids go to sleep, and just you and I go out?"

She was already shaking her head. "Sam, it's been a long day and—"

"Are you always this difficult to date?" He grinned. "Because last I checked, you kissed me back, twice, and that doesn't communicate 'not interested in dating you.'"

She let out a long sigh. "It's just...complicated."

"You said that already. A dozen times." Yet he read clear attraction between them. Unless maybe he'd been out of the game for so long that he was reading her wrong. "How is it complicated? Is there a boyfriend back in Atlanta?"

*Please say no.*

"No boyfriend. It's not that." She tore a leaf from a low-hanging branch, and watched it flutter to the ground. "I'm not staying here forever. You know that. I have to go back to Atlanta. Back to my real career."

Yeah, she did. And he didn't want to think about that day or when it would come. All he wanted to focus on was the fact that she was here now. He wanted to see more of Katie—and not with his children in the background.

And he knew the kids were getting attached to her, as much as he was. He didn't want her to leave, didn't want her to ever return to Atlanta. Maybe he'd come up with some brilliant idea that would keep Katie in Stone Gap.

"Either way, I see no reason for you and me not to have a little adult time. So before you can say no again, I'll call Della." He did just that, pulling out his cell phone and dialing Della Barlow. A few minutes of conversation and he had a babysitter lined up. "Della's going to meet us at the house in a few hours. That's just enough time to get the kids some dinner, bathed, in bed and asleep, especially after the busy day in the sun."

A smile curved across Katie's face. "You don't give up easily, do you?"

"Nope. Not in real estate and not—" he turned to her and tipped a finger under her chin "—when it comes to beautiful and stubborn women."

Katie had opted to go back to the bed-and-breakfast to get changed, so Sam could have some alone time with his kids, and to give herself a few moments to process how she'd gotten swept up into agreeing to dinner tonight. She should keep her distance, but there was something about his smile that drew her even when she knew he was the kind of man who wanted a future she didn't think she could give him. Sam wanted marriage, maybe more kids.

So she'd done the only thing she could think to do— she'd checked her email to see if anyone in Atlanta was looking for a CPA. And there in her in-box were two job offers, both at firms she knew and liked. Which meant she had a decision to make—to stay or go back.

Either way, it was crazy to even consider something long-term with a man she had just met. Sam was the kind of guy a woman settled down with, living in a tiny town like Stone Gap, in the house with a fenced-in yard and a playful golden retriever. For a moment, she'd thought she was that kind of woman.

She wasn't even sure if she had it in her to risk all that again. To dream about a forever kind of life with a husband and kids, and in the end, see both taken away in a blink.

"You look beautiful," Della said, when Katie came into the kitchen a little while later. "I'm so glad you and Sam found a way to go out. As disappointed as I am that I won't get to spoil those two little munchkins of his, I understand him wanting to spend time with his kids before they go to bed. Those little-kid years disappear in the blink of an eye. I love my granddaughter, Maddy, to pieces, and can't wait for my sons to bless me with more grandchildren to spoil."

Katie sat down at the kitchen table, a space that already felt like home, even after little over a week. She loved this bed-and-breakfast, with its warm tones and fresh-baked-bread scent. "Can I ask you something, if it's not too forward?"

"Honey, I was raised by a woman who believed in living out loud. My mama, bless her heart, never let the sun rest without telling folks how she felt, or giving them advice they may or may not have asked for." Della smiled. "There's nothing you can say or ask me that I'm going to think is too forward."

Katie toyed with the edge of the red plaid place mat, her finger running along the woven edge. "How do you know if you're ready to settle down with one person?"

"I don't know if anyone ever feels ready to settle down," Della said. "It's a scary thing to do, because it means you're giving your heart to just one person, and trusting that they aren't going to break it."

Della's gaze took on a faraway look, and Katie wondered if she was thinking about the brief affair her husband had had, the one that had produced Colton. As

much as Katie adored Della Barlow, she was grateful
for her brother's existence.

"I never thought I'd want to have that white-picket
life," Katie said. "My childhood was…rough, and I had
decided when I was young that instead of settling down,
I was going to work on my career and never end up like
my mother. Then I had a chance at the very life I had
avoided and…even though I…I lost it, it made me wish
for that one thing."

Della's features softened with understanding. It was
as if there was some unspoken language among women,
where they knew the pain the other had gone through.
"And you're scared to take that risk again, in case the
same thing happens."

Tears burned the back of Katie's eyes. It was all she
could do to nod.

"Life is about risk, honey." Della's warm hand covered Katie's. "You risk your heart and sometimes it gets
broken, but sometimes it finds the greatest love you
will ever know. A love that can withstand the harshest
storms. A love that is there for you, especially when you
suffer a loss you think you can't ever get past." Della's
words seemed to come from a place deep inside her, a
place of shared hurt.

"Did you lose a baby, too?"

Della nodded, and her eyes misted. Even all these
years later, the pain still flickered on her face. "It was
my second pregnancy. Mac was only a few months old,
and when I got pregnant again right away, a part of
me—" she swallowed, paused a moment "—a part of
me was resentful. I had my hands full with my first
baby, and all I can remember is feeling so overwhelmed,
and thinking how on earth will I do this with two babies? Then a little over a month later, I woke up in the

worst pain I'd ever felt, and I thought…" She took in a deep breath, held it for a moment. "I thought God was punishing me for wishing I wasn't pregnant. My Bobby was there for me, thank God, and we got through it, together. For a long time, I felt like a failure because my body had betrayed me."

"That's how I feel, too." The knowledge that she wasn't the only one feeling that way eased the ache in Katie's heart. "This is the one thing all women can do, and I…couldn't."

"It wasn't you, honey. It was just part of nature's plan. It took me a long time to work up the courage to try again, but I am so grateful I did, because I have Jack and Luke. Those boys are the best part of my life, and the family I've formed with Bobby is the only legacy I really care about leaving." Della got to her feet, leaned over and drew Katie into a short, tight hug.

"Take the risk, Katie. In the end, even if it doesn't work out, you will be stronger and better for it. And your life will have a meaning you can't find punching a time clock."

Tears sprang to Katie's eyes. This woman she barely knew was more of a mother than her own had ever been. Katie's arms went around Della and she leaned into the hug. It was as warm and comforting as the sunny yellow kitchen and the fresh baked bread on the counter.

After a long time, Della drew back and gave Katie a watery smile. "You have a wonderful time with Sam tonight. He's a good man, one of the best. And if you take a chance on him, you may just find the very thing you've been seeking all your life."

"What's that?"

Della's hand cupped Katie's jaw, and her big green eyes held pools of understanding. "A home."

## Chapter Ten

Sam stood on the front porch of the Stone Gap Inn, as nervous as he had been in ninth grade when he'd gone to Amy Jean Mollering's house to ask her to the freshman dance. Tonight, he'd nicked himself shaving, spent a solid ten minutes looking for a belt, and nearly walked out of the house without his shoes.

After watching "Frozen," taking baths and hearing three stories, the kids had finally fallen asleep. Henry had curled up in Sam's arms as he'd read a book about pirates, but Libby had stayed on the end of the bed, like an island of one. Still, she had stayed through both books Henry picked, then requested a favorite of hers from years before—a story about a princess living in a forgotten castle. Sam had taken that as a good sign. Maybe things were turning in a better direction with his kids. Maybe he could find a way to balance everything.

All that optimism faded the minute he reached the

front steps of the Stone Gap Inn. It was insane to be this nervous about taking a woman he had already spent an entire day with out on a date. But it was the first time he'd been entirely alone with a woman in a long time, and he wasn't quite sure he remembered how this whole dating thing worked. Surely in the ten years since he'd married Wendy, the rules had changed. Somebody really should hand out a manual, because Sam didn't have a clue. And the friend he would most likely ask for advice was Katie's brother. Probably not the best resource for how to woo this particular woman.

There was still a lingering feeling of guilt in his chest. It wasn't just about how he began to date again, but whether he *should*.

He rang the bell, and Mavis Beauchamp pulled open the door a moment later.

"Well, if it isn't Sam Millwright!" Mavis exclaimed. She opened her arms and drew him into a tight hug. "I haven't seen you in months, young man."

"Evenin', Mrs. Beauchamp."

She drew back and assessed him, an ample hip cocked to one side, her bright floral housedress looking like a garden exploded. "And what brings you by?"

"I'm here to call on Katie." There was just something about being around Mavis that made a man revert to the more formal language of the old South. Maybe it was the way she was so deeply rooted in the traditions of this area, or the way she looked at folks, as if expecting them to trot out their Sunday best on a Tuesday afternoon.

"Oh, yes, Della said something about that, just before she headed out the door. You come right on in and make yourself comfortable. I'll go get Katie." Mavis ushered him into the front parlor and waved him toward a rose-colored love seat. "Do you want some iced tea? Lemonade?"

"I'm fine, ma'am, thank you."

"All right. I'll be back faster than a squirrel can shake his tail." She gave him a wave, then headed down the hall. He heard Mavis in the kitchen, telling Katie her gentleman caller had arrived, and Sam had to bite back a laugh. He didn't think he'd ever been referred to as a gentleman caller in his life.

He rose as Katie entered the room. She'd changed since their day at the beach, and wore a light blue dress that flared at the waist and danced around her calves. Her long brown hair hung in loose waves around her shoulders, and she'd done something different with her eye makeup, because her eyes seemed even bigger and browner. "You look beautiful," he said.

She blushed. "Thank you."

"I know we already ate, so I thought maybe we could head to one of my favorite places in Stone Gap."

"Where's that?"

He grinned. "It's a surprise."

"Don't you dare take Katie to Makeout Hill," Mavis called from the kitchen. "No lady should be sitting in the backseat of your car, getting busy."

Sam laughed. "Don't worry, Mrs. Beauchamp. I'm not a getting-busy-in-the-backseat kind of guy."

"Uh-huh. I don't know about that. Most every man I know is a getting-busy kind of guy." Mavis poked her head into the front parlor. "You two get on out of here before I shoo you out. I have things to do, and I can't be standing around, visiting all night."

Sam laughed again, then put out his arm to Katie. "I think that's our cue."

She slipped her hand in the crook of his elbow. "Good night, Mavis. Don't wait up."

"You know I will." Mavis waved them off, then headed back to the kitchen.

Sam led Katie out to his car, opened the door for her, then waited for her to settle into the seat before going around to the driver's side. Once he was behind the wheel, the nerves returned, so he defaulted to the common ground of talking about the kids. "Even after that day at the beach, I ended up reading three stories to the kids before they finally fell asleep. Even Libby requested a book she used to love when she was little. It's the first time she's done that in a long, long time."

"That's wonderful," Katie said.

"I think Della was a little disappointed that the kids were asleep when she got there," he said.

Katie laughed. "She wanted to spoil them. She's one of the most motherly people I've ever met, especially with the guests at the inn. I have hot coffee and warm fresh bread waiting on a tray outside my room every morning. And there are always fresh cookies in the kitchen, and heck, even the linens smell like lilacs."

"She's the mom everyone wishes they had, even the people that had cool moms." He liked Della, liked all the Barlows, in fact. They were a great family and had made Stone Gap proud.

He started the car, then pulled away from the curb. Night was falling and the streetlights winked on, one by one, as he headed away from the bed-and-breakfast.

"I don't know about you but I'm crazy nervous," Katie said.

He laughed. "You read my mind. Maybe it's because it's been a while since I dated, or maybe it's because you work for me—"

"But this feels a little weird." They both nodded. "Then how about we don't call it a date? Just…getting together. Nothing more."

Not calling tonight a date kept him from feeling like this was wrong—too soon, too much, too something for a man widowed only a year and a half ago. Though a part of him wondered if he was using those feelings as a way to not deal with the fact that he did, indeed, want very much to date Katie. "Okay, it's not a date. Technically."

"Good." She sat back in her seat. "So…where are you taking me on our not-date?"

"If I told you, it wouldn't be a surprise, now would it?" He turned left, then right, winding his way out of the neighborhoods near Stone Gap's downtown area. The house-lined streets gave way to more trees, fewer residences, and then finally to a long stretch of woods that nearly swallowed the moonlight above. He took another turn, down a rutted road, and pulled to a stop beside a decaying house that had stood on this land for so long nobody in town could remember who had first owned it. He parked the car and turned off the engine. "This is my favorite place in all of Stone Gap."

"This…place? But it's…"

"A piece of crap," he finished. "Yup. But it's a piece of crap with serious potential. Come on, let me show you."

He grabbed a flashlight from the glove compartment, got out of the car, then came around to her side and took her hand as she exited. She'd worn flats with her dress, which was a good thing, because the terrain by the house was rough. "It still has good bones," he said as they walked up the slope of the bumpy driveway, their path illuminated by the flashlight's beam. "And one hell of a view."

Sam led Katie up the porch steps and around to the back of the house. At the base of the hill, Stone Gap Lake spread its deep, dark waters before them like a man offering his palm. The moon caught the slight ripples and bounced off them in tiny sparkles. A loon called from somewhere far across the lake, a lonely cry that echoed in the quiet.

"It's beautiful," Katie said, her voice so soft the word was almost a breath. "Absolutely beautiful."

"When I was a kid, I'd come here after school, and just sit on the porch and do my homework and watch the lake. The birds diving for their lunch, the fish splashing away, the fishermen whiling away an afternoon. It was peaceful and quiet. I used to imagine that when I grew up, I'd buy this house and live here with a dozen kids of my own."

"Why didn't you?"

He shrugged. "Wendy wanted the subdivision life. She wanted the neighbors and the block parties and the sidewalks. So we lived in a neighborhood. But this house…it was always the one I wanted my kids to live in, so they could run in the yard and fish in the lake and swing on a rope swing."

Katie spun in a slow circle, taking in the rest of the lake view, the woods to the left, the long empty field to the right. "Who owns it now?"

"An overwhelmed commercial Realtor with two mortgages and two kids."

She turned back to him, her jaw agape. "You bought it, after all?"

He still remembered the day he'd passed papers on this old home, thinking he'd finally have his dream.

He'd been so excited to hand his wife the keys, to start taking the first steps toward their new future together. "I thought I'd surprise Wendy on our fifth anniversary. Libby was four, and I thought it was a great time to move out of the subdivision and into a great old house like this one. We rarely fought, but boy, did we fight that day. I finally agreed to sell this house, but in the end, I just couldn't do it. The mortgage isn't much, because the house isn't worth much, so I kept on paying for it, and we kept on arguing about it."

"I think it's a fabulous place." Katie walked down the back porch stairs, ignoring the creak of the old, faded wood. She spun in a circle again, drinking in the expansive view, the carved columns, the wide plank floors, illuminated by Sam's flashlight. "I lived in the city all my life. Cramped little apartments in concrete prisons. I would have loved to have grown up somewhere like this. Heck, I'd love to *live* somewhere like this even now, as an adult."

That made a little part of Sam happy. He had hoped Katie would have that reaction, but wasn't sure she would love this run-down old house like he did. He'd been toying with the idea of hiring Colton's sister-in-law-to-be, Savannah, who was engaged to Mac Barlow, to look at restoring the house. He'd seen some of Savannah's restoration work—including the Stone Gap Inn—and been very impressed. "Do you want to see the rest of the place?"

"I'd love to."

He put out his hand as they walked into the house, and when she slid hers into his palm, the touch felt right. Perfect. With the flashlight illuminating the way, they walked hand in hand through the rooms, and Sam told her the plans he had for the place. All these years of thinking about how he would restore the old house had filled his mind with dozens of ideas, and he rattled them off like a locomotive racing down the tracks.

They moved from the parlor to the dining room. Floor-to-ceiling windows looked out over the fabulous view out back. The previous owner had started to renovate the house more than twenty years ago, and stopped after the demolition stage, which left gaping holes in several places, and more than a few walls stripped back to the frame. But Sam could still see his vision, could imagine the house with all the changes he wanted to make. "I want to put a coved ceiling in the dining room and a chandelier in the center. There's a space there for a built-in hutch, and I think it would look awesome if I had one with a glass front, and opened the back to the kitchen on the other side. The wainscoting is still in great shape, and I think it all can be salvaged. If not, I know Savannah has a whole garage filled with pieces she's scavenged over the years."

"These wide plank floors are incredible," Katie said, toeing the hardwood beneath her feet. "Are you going to save them?"

"As best I can. There's some water damage in the kitchen, and one of the upstairs bedrooms had a roof leak that pretty much destroyed all the flooring and walls. I did a temporary patch on the roof, but it really needs to be redone."

She let out a low whistle. "That all sounds pretty expensive."

"It is. But if I can wrap up this mall occupancy project that I'm working on, the commission from that should be enough to get the changes started here." He ran a hand through his hair and wrestled with the same internal debate he'd been having for a year and a half.

Was the smartest plan starting over here? He'd always imagined his kids playing in the big yard, running through the water, hanging pictures on the long wall in the kitchen. He'd imagined notching their heights in the wooden molding around the doors, setting a Christmas tree in the foyer by the bay window...

"I just don't know if I want to uproot the kids and move them someplace else," he said. "All their memories of their mother are in that other house."

"No, they're not, Sam. They're here." Katie placed a hand on his chest, right above his heart. Her palm spread warmth through the layer of his shirt. "They're in Tuesday night ice cream dinners and the same bedtime story every night and even George the bear. If you talk to the kids, I think you'll find that they remember a lot about their mother. A lot of things that they want to talk about, too."

Libby had barely talked about her mother since she died. Henry hadn't talked at all. The last thing Sam wanted to do was make any of this harder on them. "I guess I thought if I brought up old memories, it would make them upset. Losing her was so hard on them, and the last thing I wanted to do was bring that pain to life again."

Katie left her hand on his heart, a delicate, comforting touch. "They want to share those memories, and I think they need to. And I think as long as you do that, it won't matter what house you live in."

He covered her hand with his own and smiled down at her. This woman seemed to know exactly what to say, and exactly when to say it. With a few sentences, she'd eased his doubts and fears. "How did you get so wise?"

"I read a lot of romance novels." She grinned.

"And in those novels, is the hero always rescuing the heroine?"

"Sometimes it's the opposite." She smiled wider, and her gaze dropped to their joined hands. Neither of them spoke for a moment.

The tension in the air began to thicken, shifting from comfort to something different. Something warmer. He wanted to act on it, wanted to kiss her, wanted more. But still he hesitated. This date/not-date they were on was still in an undefined limbo.

Holding tight to her hand, he lowered their clasped palms to his side. "Come on, I want to show you the kitchen."

He led her down a short hall and into the kitchen. It was a big room, fourteen by eighteen, with a hearth at one end and a long island at the other. The upper cabinets were missing, but the sink was still there, and he'd brought over two bar stools to set on either side of the island.

In the center were two candles and a vase of fresh flowers. He had bought sandwiches and one of those ready-made dessert plates from the grocery store filled with little bites of brownies, chocolate-covered strawberries and a few cookies. And a bottle of wine, flanked by two glasses, was chilling in a bucket of ice. He leaned over, lit the candles, and stepped back.

"Oh, Sam, when did you do all this?" Her hand squeezed his a little tighter, and Sam's heart lifted.

"On my way over to pick up you. I didn't know what kind of wine you liked, so I went with a chardonnay. I hope that's okay. I bought ham-and-cheese and turkey-and-cheese sandwiches, so you could choose." God, he sounded nervous.

"It all looks amazing. Thank you."

He pulled out one of the bar stools and made a sweeping gesture. "Best seat in the house, mademoiselle."

She laughed and slid onto the bar stool, then laid a napkin across her lap. He took the seat across from her, then divvied up the sandwiches and poured them each a glass of wine. The sexual tension was still there between them, playing like background music to the food and conversation. "So what made you get into real estate?" she asked, then took a bite of her sandwich.

"I was always fascinated with buildings when I was a kid," he said. "I thought about becoming an architect or a contractor, but then I met Wendy, and her uncle was a Realtor. He let me go along with him a few times and see how it worked. I loved the challenge of marketing a property, finding the right buyer, or discovering that one forgotten piece of real estate that's just perfect for a client. I still do love that part." He took a bite of his sandwich, chewed and swallowed. "So why did you become an accountant?"

"Well, not because I loved it." She let out a little laugh. "I was good at math in school. I liked the order of it, how everything would align just right. My guidance counselor suggested I look at accounting schools, and the first one I applied to offered me a scholarship, so I took it. I just...wanted to get out of there. Colton was working at the fire station, and I didn't want to live at home anymore. So I took the scholarship, and ended up as a CPA."

"Order in chaos." He nodded. "I can understand that. You did the same with the kids, you know. Things were kind of a mess before you came along."

She ran a finger along the rim of her wineglass and watched the shimmer of the white wine in the dim candlelight. "I think it's because I could relate to them," she said. "Colton and I bonded together, because our mother was absent. And I think after they lost their mom, Henry and Libby bonded, too."

"They did. I was working, and grieving myself, and I wasn't there as much as I should have been." He sighed. "I wish I could do all those months over again."

"You're doing it right now, Sam. That's what's important."

"With your help." He covered her hand with his own. "You have made everything better, Katie. I can't thank you enough."

She shook her head and glanced downward. "Just doing my job."

"Is that all it is? A job?"

She lifted her gaze to his. A moment passed, another. The thread between them tightened again, shifting like the winds. "No. It's more than that."

The words made him happy. Made him forget all the reasons this wasn't supposed to be a date. Made him think again how beautiful she looked, how alone they were, and how very much he wanted to kiss her. Hell, he'd wanted to kiss her from the minute he met her, and now that he had, he knew how sweet and wonderful it would be.

He got to his feet and took the empty paper plates from their sandwiches to toss in the trash. "Which dessert would you like? There's cheesecake, brownies, chocolate-covered strawberries. I didn't know what you liked, so I bought them all."

She looked up at him and smiled, a wide, breathtaking smile that hit him hard. She held his gaze for a heartbeat, and the tension between them coiled even tighter. She shifted her weight in his direction and entwined her fingers with his. "I like pretty much all wine, and as for dessert, I love anything that has chocolate on it."

"Anything?"

The smile on her face eased into one that held flirtation. The desire that Sam had managed to keep on low all day flared up a few notches. "Anything," she whispered.

He leaned over and scooped a dollop of chocolate onto his index finger, then placed it against her lips. They parted, and her tongue darted out and tasted the sweet icing, then ate the bite. Her gaze never left his, and he had to resist the urge to groan. He moved his hand away and kissed her, this time hard and fast, tasting the chocolate on her tongue.

She pressed against him, fitting perfectly in his arms. His hands roamed down her back, over her buttocks, up her sides. She clutched at his shirt, drawing him closer, hungry for him, as hungry as he was for her. He wanted to hitch up her dress and have her right here, right now, on the kitchen counter, but instead he scooped her into his arms and headed out of the kitchen.

She let out a giggle and tightened her grip on him. "Where…where are we going?"

"Not all the bedrooms were damaged by the rain." His gaze met hers, half question, half invitation. Did she want this to go further as much as he did? Had she been feeling that same fire between them?

A sexy smile curved across her face. "I'm very glad to hear that."

He kicked open one of the bedroom doors. Years ago, he'd put a bed in here, intending to have a place to rest when he was working on the house, or to spend the weekend if he took the family fishing at the lake, but he'd never really used it. Tonight, he was damned grateful to have that bed there.

He laid Katie on the queen mattress and stepped back to look at her. She was beautiful in the moonlight streaming through the windows, casting her features with a soft pale wash. He lay down beside her and traced a line from her neck to her belly, over the hills of her breasts, down the valley of her abdomen. "You are incredible," he whispered.

"And you are biased." But she smiled all the same.

She reached for his shirt, but he took her hand and stopped her. "I mean it. From the minute you arrived on my doorstep in those heels and that skirt, I have known you were different. Unique. Special."

"I thought the same about you. The handsome widower trying so hard to get it right."

He grinned. "You think I'm handsome?"

"Let me show you the answer to that question." She untucked the tail of his button-down shirt and slid a hand against the smooth skin of his chest, then reached over with her other hand to unfasten the buttons.

Damn. He'd thought he wanted her before, but when she took the lead like that it sent his pulse into overdrive. Sam wrangled his arms out of his shirt and tossed it to the side, then reached for the hem of her dress. She arched up on the bed, and he slid the dress up and over her, then threw it to wherever his shirt had landed.

His gaze traveled over her, drinking her in. She had on white lace panties and a white lace bra that cupped her perfect breasts. Her belly was flat, toned, and he ran his palm over the taut expanse of skin, sliding one finger under the edge of her bra, toying with the edge of her breasts. Desire darkened her gaze and danced along her smile.

Sam traced the outline of her face. "From the minute you showed up on my doorstep, overdressed and over-qualified, I started falling for you."

She hesitated, stilling beneath him. "Falling for me? Sam, we're not—"

He placed a finger over her lips. "Not talking about any of that right now. Let's just be here, with each other."

Her hand slipped between them and slid over his erection. "That sounds like a good plan."

"Just remember I'm a little rusty." He slid his palm beneath the lace cup of her bra and caressed her breast, letting his thumb trace a circle over her nipple.

She moaned and rose up into the touch. "I wouldn't, uh, call you...rusty at all."

He slid his hand into her panties and touched her sensitive center. That made her moan even more, and buck up against him, her body begging for more. She reached for the button on his shorts, but fumbled un-doing the fastener. Her cheeks flushed, which he found adorable and sexy all at the same time. "Maybe I'm the rusty one," she said.

"Then we can be rusty together." He flicked open the button and slid down his zipper. Before he kicked his shorts to the side, he tugged a condom out of his wallet. Then he removed his boxers, slid the condom on and returned to Katie's side.

He hesitated, braced over her, his eyes connecting with hers. "What is it?" Katie asked.

"It's just..." He shook his head. "I haven't been with anyone but my wife in a very long time."

"Do you want to wait?"

There was concern in her eyes, and caring. It touched him, and reminded Sam that Katie wasn't the kind of woman who would look at tonight as a fling. That it would mean something to her, just as it did to him. He didn't know what tomorrow would bring, but he was tired of letting today slip by in a blur. "I think I've waited long enough." He slid his hand beneath her panties again, and when she rose against him with a gasp, he nearly came undone. He slid off the lacy underwear, giving him full access to the hypersensitive nub. He stroked her there, slowly at first, then faster, until she was gasping and panting, and then, a moment later, an orgasm rippled through her body.

"Oh, God, Sam," she said. "If that's rusty, I can't wait to see what more practice brings."

He chuckled softly. "Me, too." With his other hand, he slid the straps of her bra down, then peeled back the lacy cups. He lowered his mouth to her neck, then kissed down the valley of her throat, across to one breast, teasing the nipple with his tongue, before giving the other the same attention.

She put a hand on his chest, her eyes wide in the dark. "Sam…"

"I know." He cupped her chin and kissed her, gently, slowly. "If we do this, it changes—"

"Everything."

He nodded. "Is that okay?"

She ran a hand over his hair, then down along the side of his jaw. A light touch, but it seemed to whisper a dozen messages. Her gaze never wavered from his, and he knew, in that look in her eyes, in the touch of her hand, that she was feeling the same powerful wave as him. "Yes," she said, the word caught on a breath.

He shifted until he was above her, then lowered himself, his elbows on either side of her head. He kissed her again, deep and slow, kissed her until she was writhing beneath him, her hands roving over his back, his legs, his buttocks. Kissed her until she was whispering his name with urgency.

He slid into her then, and she rose up to meet him, bringing her hips to his with every stroke. They fell into a perfect rhythm, matching each other move for move, building in intensity and pace, until she was gasping and calling his name and clutching at him. He sank into her, deeper this time, and his orgasm rushed over him like a tsunami.

His heart was still thudding when he rolled to the side and pulled Katie against him. She nestled in his arms, and for a moment, it seemed like everything was perfect in the world. "That was…" His brain short-circuited and his voice trailed off.

"Incredible."

"I think we're going to need a thesaurus, because *incredible* doesn't even begin to describe how amazing that was." He laughed with her, then drew her closer still and pressed a kiss to her temple. "How amazing you are."

As she curved into him and laid her head above his heart, Sam realized Katie was right. Making love had changed everything and had him desiring things he wasn't sure he had any right to desire. With a woman who had made it clear she had no intention of staying.

## Chapter Eleven

Katie lay in Sam's arms, content and warm, while the clouds played with the moon and the night birds called to each other across the lake. She wanted to stay here forever, in this old, drafty house that seemed worlds away from everything she'd ever known.

But as the minutes ticked by, reality began to settle in and remind her that she wasn't staying in this town, with this man. She was going to have to move forward. She had savings, of course, and Sam was paying her, but that didn't mean she could afford to put off the future indefinitely.

As if on cue, she heard her phone ping. Email. She rolled to the side, fished out her phone and scrolled through the messages.

Hey, Katie, got your message. We'd love to have you start right away. Can you be here Monday? We have a new client...

The job she'd been offered at one of the firms she liked and respected wanted her to start immediately. With a little bit of a pay bump. She should have been excited, but the idea of going back to working with numbers all day depressed her. She'd had more fun than she'd expected tutoring Libby, coloring pictures with Henry, teaching Libby how to sew. And then there was Sam...

Already she cared more about him than she wanted to. *From the minute you showed up on my doorstep, overdressed and overqualified, I started falling for you.*

She'd tossed back a joke to his words, because it was easier than saying the same thing had happened to her. The minute she'd seen him with his children, the way he was so tender, so sweet, she'd begun falling for him. Wanting to be more than just the tutor to his kids, the fill-in nanny. Wanting the life she had only dared to dream of once before.

And that meant she was getting way too comfortable here in Stone Gap. From the way Sam had asked her about staying, she knew he was thinking about a future between them. A future she couldn't give him.

Sam wanted to get married again. To have more kids. Katie couldn't trust her body—what if she miscarried again? What if she wasn't meant to be pregnant? What if she settled into this life, and a year from now realized she wasn't a good mother at all? She'd already be indelibly inked in the kids' lives, and pulling away after that would be so much harder, more destructive. To them, to him and to her.

Sam rose up on one elbow and trailed a finger along her nose. "Hey, what's so important that you have to be on the phone?"

She wanted to joke back, or kiss him and delay this

conversation, but that wasn't going to do either of them any good. She had to be up front and honest. Maybe then this...whatever this was between them would end, and she could move on. And so could Sam.

The mere thought of him moving on without her caused an ache deep inside Katie. That alone verified that she was in way too deep. Better to be honest now than to hurt ten times more later.

She thought of the email. The job she'd be crazy to turn down. She had everything she needed except the motivation to leave. Maybe if she said the words aloud, it would be easier to accept them. "I'm thinking about heading back to Atlanta."

His eyes clouded. "Already? But you've only been here a few weeks."

"I can't afford to be on vacation forever. I was offered a new job, with a great firm. I think it's time I... get back to my life." *Life? More like an empty apartment in a concrete high-rise in a cold gray world I never liked. My friends, who were really just work colleagues. My mother, who barely sets aside five seconds to ask how I am.*

Yeah, that life. It wasn't until Katie had arrived here, in Stone Gap, and seen the happiness in Colton's face that she realized how much she hated her life in Atlanta. She craved what Colton had found here, with the department, with Rachel, with his other family.

As for Sam...

Sam was everything she'd ever dreamed of and never believed she could have. The family man with the big heart, who tried his hardest to be the kind of person his children and spouse needed him to be. The kind of guy a girl could lean on, depend upon. Grow attached to, as well as to his kids...

And to his dream of having more of that.

The moon shone through the dusty windowpanes with a pale white haze. The light danced off the worn wainscoting and battered wood floors. This was a house with character, memories. It was no surprise that Sam wanted to build more of that here.

That wasn't who she was, wasn't the kind of life she saw in her future. She needed to accept that, and go back to her predictable days of numbers that added up just so. Instead of taking a risk on something that could very easily go wrong. Hadn't she learned that painful lesson already?

"A new job?" Sam asked. "I thought you were already a CPA, or at least you were."

"Well, I am a CPA. Just not an employed one." She drew in a deep breath. "I was sort of fired from my job when I screwed up a couple of accounts. That's not like me, but I was going through a lot of things at the time and I... I lost my focus."

It was more than losing her focus, but she didn't know how to tell Sam the rest.

He brushed a tendril of hair off her forehead. His eyes were kind, caring. "What kind of things?"

Damn it. When she looked in his eyes, she saw that he truly wanted to know, because he cared. That look nearly undid her.

She started to speak, then took in the moonlit walls and floors again. The old sleigh bed they were lying in. The home that Sam dreamed of having. If she told him about the miscarriage, about how she had fallen apart, then maybe he would stop looking at her like that, and they would end this now and she wouldn't be foolish enough to believe she could have the same dream as he did. She had no experience being a mother—heck, she had grown up without one. Sure, she could do this for a few weeks, but long term? Better to leave now, before either of them got any more wrapped up.

Yes, that was best. Or at least, that's what she told herself, even though every cell in her body was protesting and telling her to just shut up and lie here against him and soak up the moment.

Instead, she came down firmly in the middle, not telling him the truth, but not caving to her own desires. "I'll stay and help you with the kids until you find somebody else to be their nanny," Katie said. "But I think it's best that I go back to Atlanta."

"Find another nanny? You're really leaving?"

"We always knew this was temporary. You need someone else, and I don't want to leave you short-handed." She averted her gaze from his because she couldn't stand to see the hurt and confusion in his eyes.

"What about us?"

The three words hung in the air, and for a second, Katie wanted to undo everything she had just said, turn back the clock.

"You and I want different things, Sam," she said finally, "and it's better if we don't get any closer than we already have."

His fingers dropped from her face and he drew back. "Did something happen in the last half hour that I missed? Because last I checked, we were making love and everything was great. Incredible, we both said."

It was. It had been. She wanted more, wanted this moment to last forever. But that was foolish and impractical, and if there was one thing Katie wasn't, it was that. "I shouldn't have done that, shouldn't have led you on."

*"Led me on?"*

"I wanted it as much as you did." Oh, Lord, how she

wanted that, wanted him, and still did, even now when she knew they were all wrong for each other. "But I don't want the same future you do and it's best that I tell you now and let you move on."

With someone else. The thought threatened to break her.

He didn't say anything for a moment, just stared at her as if she was a total stranger. "What are you talking about?"

"You want to get married again and have more kids." She toyed with the edge of the sheet, and wished she had waited to have this conversation when it wasn't so easy to lean into him again. They were so close she could feel the heat from his body, and oh, how she wanted to press herself to him, to make love again, to just *be* with Sam. "I'm...not the kind of woman who should do that. Who should be a mother."

"Not the kind of woman who should do that?" Sam said. "You are *fabulous* with Libby and Henry. You've created a home out of the chaos I was living in. And you've made my kids laugh and engage for the first time in forever. That says you are exactly the kind of woman who settles down and has kids."

"This is temporary, Sam," she said, even though the words scraped her throat and burned in her eyes. "And I think we should just accept that and move on in different directions."

Then before she could change her mind or undo all of what she had said, Katie sat up, swung her legs over the side of the bed and started getting dressed again. Her clothes settled into place and provided a little bit of distance, a little more of a wall.

Sam did the same, pulling on his shorts and shirt, then tugging the sheets back into place on the bed.

There was a cold divide between them now, erasing the blissful moment earlier. Oh, how she wished she could erase the last few minutes, but that would just make leaving that much harder.

"I guess I'll drive you home, then," Sam said.

"Thank you."

It was all very distant and icy, and Katie told herself that was exactly what she wanted. But as they passed by the kitchen and she saw the simple tableau of flowers, wine and dessert, her heart broke. She started to reach for his hand, but at the last second grabbed her purse instead and clutched it to her chest. The cold leather was no substitute for what she really wanted.

It wasn't until she was back in her bedroom at the bed-and-breakfast that Katie allowed herself to cry. She cried until her pillow was damp and the ache in her heart became a dull pain.

Sam couldn't concentrate. It took him five tries to dial the number of a longtime client, six attempts at sending an email before he finally typed it without mistakes. His mind kept reaching back to last night, to Katie's sudden 180.

Everything had been going so well, and then wham, out of nowhere she was talking about leaving. It wasn't as if he had expected her to stay here forever...

Okay, so maybe a part of him was thinking she'd love Stone Gap and the kids and working for him so much that she would stay. And he could date her, and maybe, just maybe find the future he never thought he could have again.

Realistically, he'd known deep down inside that she'd have to go back to Atlanta someday. She'd mentioned it a couple times before, but he hadn't really listened—or hadn't wanted to listen.

Only an idiot thought a CPA would be happy as a nanny, along with the drastic pay cut the job entailed. Of course she'd want to go back to her career, and it only made sense to return to the place where all her contacts lived, making it easier to find a new job. But still...

Lunchtime rolled around, and Sam debated going home and seeing Katie and Henry. Then a text from Colton asked if he wanted to meet the Barlow boys for lunch downtown, and Sam said yes. Maybe a few minutes with Colton would pull Sam out of this distracted mood. Or maybe a part of him was hoping her brother would give him a little insight into Katie's mind.

Colton was already sitting at a table for five when Sam arrived. He dropped into the chair beside Colton and put his phone in the space beside his plate. Hopefully, five minutes would go by without a call or text. "Hey, Colton, how are you?" Sam asked.

"Doing great. Making wedding plans with Rachel. I know more about calla lilies and tulle than any man should." He grinned that goofy grin that only a man in love would wear.

"That's great." Sam clapped him on the shoulder. "I'm happy for you."

"Thanks. She's amazing." Colton took a sip of his coffee. "Speaking of amazing women, is it true you're dating my sister?"

Direct and to the point. Sam couldn't avoid the question any more than he could avoid Colton's probing gaze. Protective older brother to the rescue.

"We...spent time together," Sam said, since he wasn't quite sure if last night qualified as a date. And considering she'd already essentially ended things between them, it wouldn't be fair to call it dating.

Except a part of him had been dating her and still wanted to. The same part that ached right now like he'd lost a limb.

Colton arched a brow. "Della says you two have spent lots of time together."

Sam scowled. That was the problem with small towns. Everyone knew everything. "Okay, yes, we went out last night. Then she told me she has to go back to Atlanta soon."

"Yup. Not surprising my little sister panicked when you got close." Colton sipped his coffee and took a few minutes to speak again. "One thing you should know about Katie—she's strong on the outside, but soft as a marshmallow inside. She had a tough life growing up, and I think that makes her scared to settle down. Hell, I was scared, too, until I met Rachel."

Sam nodded. "She told me a little about her childhood."

"It was rough." Colton waved off the waitress's offer of a refill. "Our mother wasn't the motherly type at all. She would often forget to pick Katie up from school or leave her behind at the store, or just plain ignore her. I did my best to pick up the slack, but you know, I was the older brother and a kid myself. I had my own things going on. I wish I'd done more, been there more." He sighed.

"Katie thinks you're awesome," Sam said. The close relationship between brother and sister was obvious. It made Sam miss Dylan. Maybe it wasn't too late to patch things up with his wayward brother. "Katie has had nothing but the best things to say about you."

Colton ducked his head, a small smile on his face. "Thanks. That means a lot."

"No problem." Praise from guy to guy was always an awkward thing, so Sam studied the menu for a moment while Colton drank some coffee and the moment ebbed.

Sam half expected Colton to say something like "How about those Pacers?" but instead he returned to the subject of his sister. "Deep in her heart, my sister really wants the white-picket-fence life. She even came close to having it once. But then she got her heart broken, and things sort of…fell apart for her. If you ask me, that's made her twice as gun-shy," Colton said. "She'd kill me for talking about her, but I think you're good for her, and I'd hate to see anything mess that up."

*Things sort of…fell apart.* Whatever those things were, Sam was pretty sure it was part of Katie's reluctance to get involved, her breaking it off. "It's too late. She broke up with me and is definitely going back to Atlanta."

Colton let out a long sigh. "Between you and me, I think she hates living in Atlanta, and I think living here would be great for her."

"But…?" Sam prompted, when Colton paused.

"But if she's scared, she's going to run and hide in her work or something else. All I'm saying is don't give up on her, okay? She's been through a lot, and some of that was fairly recent."

Before Sam had a chance to respond or ask what Colton meant by that, Colton's brothers ambled in and dropped into the other three chairs. Mac, Luke and Jack all had the same dark hair and blue eyes as Colton, and except for the few differences that age brought to their features, they could have passed as quadruplets. "Now we know your standards have dropped, Sam, if you're hanging around with this character." Jack gave Sam a gentle slug on the shoulder.

"Hey, hey," Colton said. "Who says it's not my standards that have dropped since I got you three as brothers?"

Luke grinned. "Because we're the cool ones."

Sam scoffed. "That was in high school." Luke had been the quarterback, Jack the popular one and Mac the high achiever. Sam had been the geeky one in band and architecture classes. The Barlow boys had always been good guys, though, even in high school.

Luke laughed. "True. Glory days are behind us and all that. How are you doing, Sam?"

"Good, good." Sam didn't get into the emotional roller coaster he'd ridden in the months after his wife died. They were guys. They talked *around* things instead of *about* them.

The men exchanged small talk for a little while, talking about their jobs, football and the Yankees chances of making it to the World Series this year. Mac talked about his plans for the solar company he was running with his fiancée, Savannah, and Luke bragged about the painting his daughter, Maddy, had exhibited in the school art show. Jack got the most ribbing, for his life as a newly married man and the little house by the lake that he was fixing up for him and Meri to live in. She was just getting her photography company off the ground, working some with Rachel, who was back to doing wedding planning while she worked part-time at her father's hardware store and planned her own wedding to Colton.

Sam marveled at how well all the brothers got along, how the entire Barlow family seemed to bond with each other, as did their wives. He missed his brother, and made a mental vow to track Dylan down and find a way to get together soon. Dylan rarely lingered in one spot, and his contact with his family was sporadic at best.

"Thanks for sending your sister to the Stone Gap Inn," Mac said to Colton. The mention of Katie drew Sam's mind back to the conversation. "Our mother's really got her heart set on making that place work."

"The house looks amazing," Sam replied. "Savannah did a great job on the restoration, and you all made quick work of getting the carpentry work done."

"We did when they listened to me," Jack said, giving his brothers the leadership look he'd perfected in the military. "Somebody had to be in charge of the clown show."

"Hey! As the family prankster, I resent that remark." Luke grinned to show he was joking, then got to his feet and tossed a couple dollars on the table for his drink. "Anyway, I'd love to stay and eat, guys, but I have to get back to the garage. I promised Peyton I'd get home early tonight. Maddy is at a sleepover and that means…" Luke's grin widened.

"That means he's ditching us in favor of his woman," Mac said.

"Duh. She's cuter than all of you put together." Luke waved goodbye, then headed out the door.

Sam's phone started buzzing, with a request for a showing from a potential client. He paid for his lunch, promised the Barlows he'd catch up another time, then headed out to the mall space. He tried not to care that Katie had texted only once, to let him know she'd picked Libby up at school.

He shouldn't let his mind dwell on a woman who was leaving, even if the thought of her doing that caused a fissure in his heart. Maybe if he focused on his job, on making those deals happen for the new mall, it would dull that ache.

A little part of him whispered that pouring his energy into work was exactly what had gotten him here in the first place. Maybe it was time for a new approach.

Or maybe he was just dreaming of things that were already too far to reach.

## Chapter Twelve

The honeymoon period had come to an end.

Libby stood in the kitchen, her arms crossed over her chest. "You aren't my mommy. You can't make me do my homework."

Katie sighed. They'd been having this argument for twenty minutes now, ever since Libby got home from school. She'd stormed out of the car, stomped into the house and slammed the door. And had started arguing as soon as Katie mentioned the word *school*. "My job, Libby, is to help you with your homework."

"No, your job is to watch Henry and me. My father said so. Because you're the nanny."

"Well, yes, that's my job, too. I have two jobs." She gestured toward the math papers on the kitchen table. "Now, come on, let's get these worksheets done and then you can go play. Or maybe after your homework is done, we could walk downtown and see the new dance studio that opened up. I heard they have ballet lessons."

"I don't care."

Katie sighed again. "Libby, listen. You have to do your homework no matter what. If I help you, then we can do the hard parts together. And then—"

"No! I said no!" Then she spun on her heel and ran out the door.

Katie glanced over at Henry, who was standing on the living room carpet, George the bear clutched to his chest, his eyes wide. Katie debated going after Libby and decided maybe it would be best to give the girl a few minutes to cool down. She thought of texting Sam, but she was on a strict no-Sam diet, to try to ease the pain in her chest every time she thought of him.

So far, that wasn't working. Being in his house, around his kids, was a constant reminder that soon she would leave all this behind. Probably for good. It would be for the best, she told herself, because she wasn't cut out for this white-picket-fence life. She may have been a decent nanny for a few days, but everything in Katie said that long-term, she didn't have the first clue how to be a good parent. She had virtually no parenting role models, and the one chance she'd had at being a mother—

Was over before it began.

Outside, Libby sat on the swing, toeing back and forth, her head down, her gaze on the ground. Katie fixed Henry a snack, then turned on his favorite television show and went outside to Libby, leaving the patio door open so she could hear Henry.

"Go away," Libby said, when Katie approached.

Katie sat in the second swing. It creaked under her weight but held. "So, what happened today at school?"

"Nothing."

"Something happened. I could tell the second you got in the car. You were madder than a hornet in a jar."

Libby didn't say anything, just kept pushing the swing back and forth, back and forth. In the distance, one of the neighbors started mowing his lawn. There was the sound of another school bus stopping a few houses away.

Katie kept waiting and Libby kept silent. Katie could understand. When she'd been little, she'd been slow to trust other people. Colton had been her one rock, the only go-to person she trusted. "Do you want me to get your dad?"

"He's never gonna come. He's working." Libby made a face.

"He came to the beach that day. He doesn't always work."

Libby shook her head. "He won't come."

Katie debated. Should she call Sam? Or try to handle this on her own? She glanced over at the sullen girl on the swing and decided things weren't going so well. It wouldn't hurt to call in reinforcements. She tugged her phone out of her pocket and texted Sam.

Libby had a bad day at school but won't talk to me about it. Can you swing by for a minute and maybe cheer her up?

There was no instant reply, but for all Katie knew, Sam could be driving or on the phone or meeting with a client. The best bet was to keep Libby focused on something else, until Sam could get here. "Libby, if we just get a start on your homework—"

"No! I don't want to! I want my mother to help me! Not you!" Libby pushed off from the swing and ran across the yard, then around the side of the house. Just as Katie started after her, Henry let out a wail.

Katie dashed into the house and found Henry on the floor, holding his foot. A pile of building blocks were scattered beside him. "Hey, did you step on one of those?"

Henry nodded. Tears streamed down his face. He held out his foot to Katie. She looked it over and saw an angry red mark, but no cuts or bruises. She drew him to her and gave him a little hug. "It looks okay," she said. "We just have to pick these up, so no one gets hurt, okay?"

She had stepped on those tiny little buggers more than once and knew the pain Henry was feeling. She reached over and scooped most of the blocks into the bin. Henry picked up a few and proudly dumped them on top of Katie's pile. "Henry help."

"You did indeed. Thank you. Now, let's go get Libby." Hopefully, a few minutes alone had calmed Libby down. Katie got to her feet, hoisted Henry onto her hip, then at the last second grabbed the bear, too, and pressed him into Henry's arms. She headed out the back door and around the side of the house.

Libby wasn't there. Katie skirted to the front of the house. "Libby?"

No response. She passed the flowerpots, then checked the other side of the house and the backyard once more. She'd done a complete tour of the perimeter and hadn't seen Libby anywhere. Alarm raised the hairs on the back of Katie's neck. "Libby? Libby!"

No response. Panic climbed Katie's throat. She ran inside—maybe Libby had come in while she was helping Henry and she just didn't hear her. Katie checked

every room, every closet, under every bed. She called
Libby's name over and over again—

Nothing.

"Where Libby?" Henry asked. His little face was
scrunched in worry.

"She's fine," Katie said. "Just playing a game of hide-
and-seek."

"Henry play, too?"

"No, not now." That was the last thing Katie
needed—both Sam's kids missing. Surely Libby couldn't
have gone far.

Katie made another loop of the yard, then checked
inside the garage. It wasn't until she turned to check
inside again that she noticed Libby's bike was missing
from its customary place by the side door.

Katie's heart clenched. Oh, God. She had lost Sam's
daughter. She'd handled the entire thing all wrong and
now Libby was gone, and Katie didn't have the first
clue where to look.

She pulled out her cell phone and dialed Sam's number. It rang three times, then went to voice mail. Katie
dialed again, reached voice mail again. She left a message, telling Sam to call her back immediately, then followed that with a text that said the same thing.

"Come on, come on," she muttered to the silent
phone. It didn't ring, didn't ping with a message. Nothing. Katie gave Henry a smile that she hoped didn't betray the panic in her chest. Where was Libby? Nearby?
Katie hoped so. When she'd been Libby's age and run
away, she hadn't gotten far…

But that was because Colton had come after her.
Colton, who knew her almost as well as she knew her-
self, and had anticipated where his little sister might go.
Katie barely knew Libby, and hadn't a clue where the

girl might run to. Guilt knotted in Katie's chest. If she had handled this better, if she'd paid more attention...

"Henry, how about we take a little walk?"

"Libby, too?"

"We'll see Libby soon," Katie said, and as she strapped Henry into his stroller, she prayed that was true.

Sam tried to hide a smile as Ginny Wilkins, soon to be Beauregard, grabbed her fiancé's hand and let out a squeal. "This is going to be perfect, baby. Can't you just see it?"

Bernard shuffled from foot to foot. He was a slight man with a lisp, and glasses that had trouble staying on his nose. Ginny was the opposite—loud and bright in a pink dress that bloomed from her waist, and pink heels that clacked on the tile floor. She dangled a daisy-shaped purse from her forearm, and called everything either "darling" or "perfect" or "divine."

"My Bernard is opening his own boutique men's clothing store and we were so glad to hear his uncle had this mall space available right away," Ginny said. "My Bernard has such a fashion sense that I'm sure it's going to be a wild success. Don't you agree, Mr. Millwright?"

Sam didn't quite see how Bernard's striped, button-down shirt and khaki pants qualified for a fashion sense. He was wearing red-and-green-striped socks, so maybe his fashion started at the bottom and worked its way up gradually. All Sam wanted was a deal inked on the small storefront, hopefully before day's end. Bernard was Hank's nephew, after all, and keeping both his boss and his boss's family members happy would bode well for Sam's future at the firm. Even if Ginny and Bernard had been walking around the same two-thousand-square-foot space for over an hour now, debating where to put clothing racks. "I think Bernard's store will be a great addition to the mall," Sam said.

"We are just so excited about the future. We're getting married soon—in a pink wedding that people will be talking about for centuries, I'm sure—and we're building the cutest little house off of Oak Street, and opening Bernard's business venture, with his daddy's money, because, well, honey, it is the South, and the best money is old money..."

Ginny went on and on as she paced the perimeter of the store again. Bernard followed along like a lonely puppy, agreeing with everything Ginny said. Sam tried hard not to look impatient. His phone buzzed a few times, but every time he went to check it, Ginny asked another question.

"So," Sam said, after they made their seventh round of the space, "would you like to make an offer? Demand is high for this area, and there's bound to be some competition for this location, since it's right next door to an anchor tenant. I know your uncle is anxious to get all the spaces rented soon so the mall grand opening can bring a lot of business in."

Inside his pocket, he felt his phone buzz again. Probably just a reminder for his next appointment in a half hour.

"I don't know..." Ginny put a finger to her lips. She glanced at Bernard, then back at Sam. "Can we decorate however we choose?"

"Of course you can."

Sam's phone buzzed one more time, the sound feeling even more insistent. He glanced at his watch. A little after four. He was supposed to call Hank at four with a status update, but the meeting with Ginny and Bernard had run way over the time he had allotted. Maybe Hank just wanted to know how his nephew had responded to the space. Sam pulled his phone out of his pocket.

"And what did you say the rent was again?" Ginny asked.

Sam rattled off the numbers, then answered Ginny's next three questions about the lease. By the time she took a breath, another five minutes had gone by and Sam's phone had buzzed twice more. "Just one second, Miss Wilkins, I really need to check this."

Ginny sighed. "Bernard and I are on a schedule, Mr. Millwright. We have two more locations we want to look at today. His uncle assured us you would give us your undivided attention."

"Just one second. I promise." As soon as he flipped the phone over, the on-screen messages made his throat close. The room swam before his eyes and the air whooshed out of his lungs.

He needed to read only three words before he turned on his heel and ran out the door.

Libby is missing.

## Chapter Thirteen

It took all Katie had not to crumple into a sobbing puddle. She'd lost Sam's child. The one task he had given her—watch his kids and keep them safe—and she had failed. Henry sat in his stroller, playing with the stuffed bear, unaware that Katie was on the verge of a nervous breakdown.

She'd been texting Sam and calling for ten solid minutes that felt like ten hours. She was just about to call the police when her phone buzzed.

On my way. There in five.

Sam. He'd know what to do. How to find Libby. Katie texted him the address where she was—a street corner about four blocks from the house—part of an ever-widening circle she'd been walking with Henry, while she looked for Libby.

She'd figured Libby couldn't have gone too far. Maybe just to a neighbor's house? She had tried to think if Libby had mentioned any friends who lived in the neighborhood, or maybe where Charity, her old nanny, lived, but had drawn a blank. So Katie kept walking and calling Libby's name, her guilt and worry increasing with every passing second.

Sam's SUV came to a screeching stop beside them and he jumped out. "Where is she?"

"I... I don't know." The tears Katie had held back for so long began to stream down her cheeks. "We had an argument, and then I went inside and she was outside—"

"You left her *alone*?"

"She was just in the yard. She was upset about school and wouldn't talk to me," Katie said, the words jerking out of her between tears. "I tried to get her to do her homework, but she got mad and ran off, and then Henry stepped on a block and he was crying, and when I turned around, she was gone. I checked the yard, the house, but her bike is gone, and I've looked all over and I don't know what to do."

"I *trusted* you with my kids, Katie. How could you do this?"

There was fury in his eyes, recrimination in his words. He was right. She'd failed him, and now Libby could be anywhere. "I'm sorry, Sam. I'm really sorry. I didn't think she'd do this. I am so sorry." Katie felt like she couldn't say it enough. God, she'd really screwed up.

Sam gave her a harsh, stony look. He glanced down at Henry, who put out his arms. "Daddy!"

Sam unbuckled his son and held him tight to his chest for a long second. Over Henry's head, Sam's gaze met hers. Pain shimmered in his eyes.

She tried to put a hand on his arm, but he shrugged off her touch. "All right, buddy, you gotta sit back in your seat and go home with Katie."

Henry shook his head. "I wanna stay wif you, Daddy."

"You can't. I have to go get Libby. But when I get home, we'll get pizza, okay?"

That was enough to make Henry agree. He climbed back into the stroller and settled George on his lap. His gaze darted between both adults, as if he knew something was wrong, but wasn't sure what it was.

"You know where she is?" Katie said quietly, so Henry wouldn't overhear. "I tried to think like her, to try to figure out where she might go. But I just don't know Libby well enough yet."

"No, you don't." His words were curt, short, accusatory.

"I'm sorry, Sam. I—"

"Wendy knew her best. She wouldn't have—" he cut off the sentence.

The unspoken words—*Wendy wouldn't have lost their daughter.* Guilt rolled through Katie. This was exactly why she wasn't fit for this life that Sam wanted. Once Libby was home safe, Katie was going to head back to Atlanta. Let Sam find someone better suited than she was. Someone he could rely on, not a woman who had lost his child.

The only thing she could do now was help him look for Libby. "Do you want us to split up? I can search this direction and you can search—"

"You've done enough, don't you think?" He let out a gust. "I'm sorry. I'm just worried. Please, take Henry home. I'll go look for Libby. If I don't find her, I'll call the Stone Gap Police Department. Just keep an eye on my son. Okay?"

She nodded, and tried to apologize again, but Sam was already in his car and peeling away from the curb.

Sam had been unnecessarily harsh with Katie. He knew that, but he didn't have time to smooth those waters right now. He'd lashed out at Katie, not just because he was worried and scared, but because he was mad at himself.

He hadn't been here. He'd been working—again—instead of being a part of his family. He'd lost that bond he had with Libby long ago, and now he had no idea where she might have gone. He drove at warp speed through town, past the school, the ice cream parlor, the library. On any other day, Libby would have gone to one of those places. But today, something had upset her, and Sam prayed he knew his daughter well enough to guess where she might have gone.

Knew her well enough. Wasn't that what Katie had said? That she had tried to think like Libby, and couldn't, because she didn't know her well enough? Sam pulled the car to the side of the road and let out a deep breath. He could feel time ticking away, time where something terrible could happen, but he closed his eyes and centered himself, and tried to think.

What would Libby do? Where would she go? Where did she feel most safe and happy...

An idea sparked in Sam's brain. He took a left on Maple, then a right on Birch, and finally, came to a stop at the end of the road.

An old park, hardly used since Stone Gap had built a prettier, newer one closer to downtown, sat at the end of Birch Street. Once upon a time, there'd been an elementary school behind the park, but as Stone Gap's population grew, the one-story school hadn't been enough

and the town had built a new one on land donated by a
farmer who had died. The park fell into disuse, leaving
only a couple swings standing and one play structure,
built thirty years ago by men who believed in building
things to last.

The castle-shaped building was probably going to be
here long after Sam was gone. He'd played on it when
he was a kid, and Wendy had taken Libby here when
she was little. Once Henry was born, Wendy hadn't
wanted to make the drive, preferring the newer playground with its baby swings and oversize tic-tac-toe
board. Sam couldn't remember the last time Libby had
been to this park, although she mentioned it with long-
ing from time to time. Some of her best memories with
her mom were here, and for a little girl who felt lost and
alone, Sam was pretty sure this was where she'd go.

Sam got out of the car, and whispered a quick prayer
before he crossed the grassy park and headed for the
castle. Why hadn't he paid closer attention? Been there
for his daughter all these months? He'd been so locked
in his own grief that he'd missed the signs that Libby
was still hurting.

His heart filled his chest, and he prayed he wasn't
too late, that he'd come to the right place. Then he saw
a familiar pink bicycle leaning against a tree, and hope
leaped within him. He ducked his head to get inside,
then climbed a small ladder up to the top of the turret.

And there, in the center of the circular space, he
found his daughter, her knees hugged to her chest, her
shoes scuffed with dirt, tears puddling on her arms. Relief flooded Sam, and his knees buckled for a second.
*Libby. Thank God.*

He climbed the rest of the way up, then folded himself into the small space beside Libby. She flicked a

quick glance at him, then went back to staring at the picture in her hands. It was worn and creased, but Sam knew it well.

Wendy holding five-year-old Libby, their faces smushed together in the little round window of the turret. It was one of the last times they'd come to this park, before Henry was born and Wendy's time with Libby became limited. Libby had carried that picture with her ever since the funeral. Sam's heart broke a little as he saw the wrinkled edges, the faded images. "Hey, Libby Bear, you had us all worried."

She sniffled. "Sorry."

"You want to talk about it?"

She shook her head.

Sam sat there for a while, feeling helpless. This was where Wendy would have stepped in, with a soothing word or a fresh-baked cookie. His late wife had a way of getting the kids to open up, of easing their fears and worries. He lacked that ability, and worried every day that he was going to lose touch with his kids before those difficult teen years.

He could feel Libby's pain radiating off her tiny frame. He didn't know what to do with pain like that, the kind of pain that went bone-deep. Didn't know how to ease the sorrow in her heart. He'd been trying to find that answer ever since Wendy died.

But there was no Wendy here now, and there wasn't going to be. Either Sam figured this out or he was going to lose what relationship he had with his daughter.

"When I was a kid, I had a tree house," Sam said, starting with just talking. He didn't know where he was going with the story or if it would help, but it was filling the silence. He thought of his childhood, of the days when he had wanted to escape. Maybe that was part of what had driven Libby to this space, a need to escape the empty spot in the house, in her life. "Did I ever tell you that?"

Libby nodded. Sniffled some more.

"I used to play up there all the time because my little brother, your uncle Dylan, couldn't get up there. Then he got older and could climb the ladder. I didn't want to share so I told him I was too old for the tree house and stopped going up there." Sam thought of that old rickety house his father had built a long time ago. It hadn't been much, just a box with a couple holes for windows and a rope with a bucket for bringing snacks up to the fort. "But then my parents got divorced and my dad moved out. It was really hard on me, because I was the oldest. Dylan was only four, but I was nine, just a little older than you."

Libby sniffled some more, but she had shifted her head in his direction to listen. Sam took that as a good sign and kept talking.

"I had a really hard time when my dad moved out, and that tree house, well, that became the place where I would go. I'd sneak up there when Dylan wasn't around and pretend nothing was changing. I'd convince myself that when I climbed down, my dad would still be there and everything would be better than it was before." That his dad would be home, involved. During those hours in the tree house, Sam used to think his life was perfect. Then he'd go in for dinner and see the empty place at the table, or see the empty hook on the wall that used to hold his dad's keys.

The commonality wasn't lost on Sam. The very thing he had hated about his childhood—his father's absence—was part of what was hurting his own kids.

Their mother was gone, forever, and their father was buried in work. Again.

Was that why Libby was here? Was she trying to pretend her life was the way it had been before? Exactly what he had done when he was her age…

"Like when Mommy used to bring me here," Libby said, her voice nearly a whisper. "That was the best. I miss that. I miss…her."

"Me, too, kiddo." He could still see Wendy pushing Libby on the swings, or darting from tree to tree, laughing, playing tag. Libby's hair a riot of curls, spreading behind her like wings as she ran. He fingered the picture in Libby's hands. "Your mom used to love bringing you here. You know why?"

Libby shook her head.

"Because she said she loved to pretend you were both princesses. She always called you that when you were little, remember? Her princess."

Libby's eyes misted. "I remember."

He brushed a tendril of hair off Libby's forehead. "I know she misses you as much as you miss her, Libby, and if Mommy could be here, she would be."

Libby shifted closer to Sam, until her thigh brushed his. "Katie said Mommy is up in the clouds. I thought maybe if I came here, I could see her better, 'cuz I'd be up high. I wanted to talk to her and…" Libby's voice caught on a sob, and tears started rolling down her cheeks. "But I can't see her and I can't talk to her. Forever."

"You can talk to me," Sam said, his voice gentle. "I'd love it if you would, Libby. Because sometimes I need someone to talk to about Mommy, too."

She turned to him then. Her eyes were wide and round, and her lower lip trembled. "You do?"

All this time, he'd thought he was making it easier on his kids by not talking about their late mother, by keeping his emotions in check, and concentrating on moving forward. But what if all they had really needed was to know they weren't alone? That he missed Wendy, too, and that there were days when he struggled to draw that next breath, take that next step. That he saw the echo of their mother in the places they'd been, the pictures they'd taken, the memories that filled every corner of their lives. "I miss her a lot, too. I miss the way she made pancakes that looked like Mickey Mouse and how she used to pile all those pillows on the couch—"

"And Henry and I would pretend to hide under them, and make a fort with the blankets."

He remembered coming home dozens of times to blanket forts. Why had he never thought to do that with the kids, too? How did he let the busyness of life replace all those things that mattered? The pancakes and the blankets and the memories? That was what his kids had needed, what Katie had been trying to tell him, all along. "And how she would make dinner into a picnic on the living room floor. Your mommy was really great, wasn't she?"

Libby nodded, and then her chin wobbled and the tears started again. She traced the outline of Wendy's face with her finger. A tear slid off her cheek and puddled on the image. "I wish Mommy was coming back."

He heard the acceptance and the loss tied up in Libby's words. It damn near broke his heart. "I know, sweetie, I know."

"Today, at school, my teacher said…to d-draw your f-family…" Libby's words came in fits and starts, mixed with tears. "And I didn't know if I should d-draw my mommy or not 'cuz…'cuz I…I don't have one anymore."

Sam would have given anything to have Wendy climb into this castle right now and ease the loss in his daughter's heart, erase the hurt in her voice. He could feel Libby's pain as if it were his own. It wasn't fair that his precious daughter was going to grow up without her mother, that she was going to miss the proms and wedding day and graduations. He couldn't change that, couldn't turn back time, but he could open his heart, and hope that was enough.

"You should draw your mom in that picture," he said, "because she's always going to be part of our family, because she's part of you and Henry. You guys are the best part of her. The part that will forever remind everyone how amazing she was."

Libby cocked her head. "How do we do that?"

"By being exactly who you are. She was always so proud of you, Libby. And I am, too." He opened his arms. "Come here, Libby Bear."

A breeze rustled through the trees, sent leaves dancing against the walls of the fort. A soft rain began to fall, pattering on the ground below, and misting through the turret window.

Libby hesitated for a second, her eyes wide, her lower lip trembling. Then she climbed into Sam's lap and slid her arms around him. Her grip tightened, bit by bit, until she leaned her head into the valley beneath his chin. Her tears fell, dampening his shirt, blurring into the cotton stripes.

"I love you, Libby," Sam whispered. He stroked her hair and held her tight, and whispered the words over and over. "I love you."

They sat there for a long time, while the world went

on outside the castle. Birds called, rain fell and the sun marched toward the horizon.

"Can you promise me something?" Libby whispered against his chest.

If she wanted him to capture the sun right now, he'd find a way to give it to her. "Anything, baby girl."

Libby raised her gaze to his. Her eyes were puddles of shimmering tears and her breath caught on a hitch. "You're never…never gonna leave me, Daddy."

*Daddy.*

Sam's heart swelled. Libby may have her mother's smile, but right now, she had her father's eyes—wide, scared, yet still holding a sparkle of hope. That was what Sam held on to, what he would always hold on to.

*Daddy.*

How he had missed that word. He folded Libby into his embrace again, and kissed the top of her head, inhaling the soft strawberry scent of her shampoo and, he swore, traces of that innocent scent of a baby. "I'm not going anywhere, Libby. I promise." He kissed her again, and felt his own tears drop onto her curls. "I promise."

## Chapter Fourteen

She damned near paced a hole in the carpet, waiting on Sam to call or text. Every car that went by made Katie jump, every buzz from an email or Facebook notification on her phone made her heart skip a beat. And then finally, just when she was about to call the police herself...

Found Libby. On our way home. Order pizza.

Katie let out a whoop, then scooped Henry up from where he was sitting on the couch. She'd imagined all the worst scenarios, and every minute had dragged by like a century. But Libby was safe, and everything was going to be okay. "Libby's on her way home, Henry. Your dad says we should order pizza. Do you like pizza?"

Henry nodded. "Pizza!"

"Pizza it is!" Katie found the pizza place menu tacked to the fridge, ordered a couple pepperoni pizzas, then sat down with Henry to make a house out of his toy bricks, to keep him occupied and keep herself from looking out the window every five seconds.

The guilt that she had been the whole reason Sam was out looking for Libby hadn't abated. Katie had been beating herself up for the past hour. She had no business being a nanny, or staying here and pretending she could ever be what Sam wanted.

She heard the front door open, then Sam's voice. Thank God.

"Go on up and wash your face, Libby," Sam said from the hall. "Pizza should be here any minute."

There was the sound of light footsteps heading up the stairs, then Sam's heavier footfalls coming down the hall and into the living room. Katie scrambled to her feet. "She's okay?"

Sam nodded. "She's fine. She was upset because her teacher had everyone in the class draw a picture of their family. That made her miss her mom a lot, so she went to this playground Wendy used to bring Libby to when she was little. She was sitting at the top of the castle they have there, and holding a picture of her mom, because she thought maybe she'd get closer to heaven that way." He let out a long sigh and dropped into a chair. Exhaustion lined his face. "God, I was so worried."

"I'm so sorry, Sam. I didn't mean to lose track of her. She was gone so fast—"

Sam put up a hand, cutting off her words. "I'm the one who should apologize for being so harsh with you earlier. I was worried, and I took it out on you. I'm sorry."

"I completely understand."

He gave her a soft smile. "If you don't have to go anywhere right away, would you stay for pizza? I think we've all had a busy day and I know the kids would love to have you here a little longer."

Katie hesitated. She was the whole reason they were here right now. If she hadn't argued with Libby, then maybe the little girl wouldn't have run away. Maybe it was better that she just left for Atlanta tomorrow. "Even Libby?"

"You're half the reason she went where she did." He shook his head and put up a hand. "Sorry. That came out wrong. What I meant is, she said you told her that her mom was watching from up above. So when she got upset, she went to the highest place she knew to try to talk to her mom."

Katie sank onto the arm of the sofa. Sam might not realize that she was at fault for tonight, but Katie knew it. She wasn't good for this family, or this man. "I'm glad Libby went somewhere safe. I was so worried."

"Me, too." Sam's phone began buzzing. He gave it a glance, then turned it off. "Tonight, all of that can wait." He crossed the living room and sank onto the carpet. "Instead, I'm going to sit on the floor and build with Henry. What are we making, buddy?"

"A house." Henry gave a little nod of decision.

"A house, huh? Who's going to live in it?"

"Me and George." Henry stacked a couple blocks, then waited while his father added some more. "And Libby and Daddy and Katie."

Whoa. Had Katie just heard Henry right? She glanced over at Sam, who was looking up at her with a bemused expression on his face.

"Seems you can't go back to a certain city in Georgia," Sam said, "because Henry here is building you a mighty nice place to live in, right here in Stone Gap."

"I, uh, think I hear the pizza guy outside." She didn't, but she left the room anyway, to wait by the front door. Easier to do that than to answer the questions hanging in the air.

She wasn't staying here. She wasn't going to live in a house with Sam and Libby and Henry. If she'd learned anything today, it was that she definitely wasn't cut out to be a mother or a stepmother or, heck, even a nanny. She'd had one job—one solitary job—and she'd failed at it. Sam might forgive her now in the rush of relief that Libby was okay, but down the road, he'd realize that Katie was better off being in charge of tax returns instead of children.

There was a sound on the stairs behind her, and Katie pivoted, to see Libby standing on the third step from the bottom. "Hi, Katie."

"Libby. Honey, I'm so glad you're home and okay."

Libby's eyes were red from crying, but she was wearing a clean T-shirt and a smile, and that was good to see. She dropped onto the bottom step. "I'm sorry for running away."

Katie sat down beside Libby, and gave her a little shoulder-to-shoulder nudge. The whole day had felt like looking into a mirror. Katie had seen herself— that scared, lonely little girl who had gathered up her toys and headed for the street—in Libby's eyes. She understood this girl, maybe more than Libby even realized. "It's okay. I did it, too, when I was your age."

"You did?"

"Yup. I was eight years old, just like you. My mom wasn't a nice mommy like yours was, and sometimes she yelled at me and scared me," Katie said, trying to find the right words to describe a childhood that was the complete opposite of Libby's. "So I packed up my favorite stuffed animals and I ran away."

"What happened? Did your daddy find you?"

"My brother did. You met him—Colton, the firefighter. Even back then he was rescuing people." Katie smiled. She didn't want to think about what her childhood would have been like if she hadn't had Colton. "He carried me home and made me supper, and told me everything would get better. He was right. It did."

"Did you run away again?"

Technically, she had, when she'd come here. She'd run away from her fears and her problems and all the things she didn't want to think about. Running straight to a man with two kids who needed a mother. Either she was a masochist or this was some kind of message from up above about facing her fears.

"Running away doesn't fix anything," Katie said. Except Katie wasn't taking her own advice. Wasn't going back to Atlanta another form of running away? "You have to talk about what scares you, because that's the only way to make it less scary."

Yeah, she hadn't done that with Sam, had she? She hadn't told him about the miscarriage or her doubts about being a good fit for the future he dreamed of, or the real reasons she was going back to Georgia.

Libby picked at a hangnail and thought about that for a second. Her long brown hair swung forward, covering her face. "Sometimes I have a hard time talking. 'Cuz it makes me cry, and I don't like to cry."

Katie smiled. Oh, how she understood that. Her whole life had been spent trying to bring order from chaos, creating straight lines instead of emotional curves. "Honey, nobody likes to cry. But sometimes it's good for you."

Again, advice Katie should be taking herself. If she had talked and let her emotions out months ago, she probably wouldn't have screwed up at work and lost her job. She probably wouldn't have had to run away to Stone Gap. Even in the couple weeks or so that she had been here, the conversations she'd had with Colton and Della had helped.

The time with Sam, with the kids, had helped ease the loss in her heart. Katie's hand strayed to her abdomen. The loss was still there, but the pain had begun to ebb. Maybe that would make it easier to go back to Atlanta, back to work and back to her life.

Except Libby leaned in just then and gave Katie a one-armed hug and whispered, "Thank you," and Katie didn't want to go anywhere. She couldn't think of a single place on earth that was better than the bottom step of Sam's staircase, sitting beside a little girl who was a kindred spirit.

Katie reached out and hugged Libby back, and whispered the same words, except hers came with a little catch in her throat. "Thank you, Libby."

By the time the pizza arrived, life was back to normal. Henry and Libby were squabbling over a toy, the TV was playing *SpongeBob* and the dog was barking at his own shadow. Sam looked around at the mess, the noise, the kids, and thought he was one damned lucky guy.

Katie was quiet at dinner, but Sam attributed that to the kids making so much noise. After they were done with the pizza, he told them they could watch the last half of *Frozen* before they went to bed. He got to his feet at the same time Katie did. They nearly collided on their way to the sink.

He caught the scent of her perfume, watched the tick of her pulse in her throat. He'd gone from knowing she was there to being insanely aware of her presence. "Sorry," he said.

"Sorry." She laid the dirty plates in the sink and turned to box up the rest of the pizza. If she felt what he had, she gave no sign of it. The quietness from dinner lingered, and there was a distance between them now. "I should get going. Thanks for the pizza."

He had hoped maybe after tonight she would change her mind about breaking up with him, but there was nothing in Katie's demeanor or words that said she was thinking about kissing him half as much as he was thinking about kissing her.

He wanted to kick himself for yelling at her, for letting his fear and his doubts fill his words. All it had done was build a wall between them.

She started to turn away, but he laid a hand on her arm. "Stay. Please. Just give it a half hour, then it's time for the kids to go to bed and you and I can talk."

He could see the hesitation in her features, the reluctance. "I know I lashed out at you this afternoon. What happened with Libby wasn't your fault. I was worried and lost my temper. I'm sorry again." He kept his hand on her arm, thinking how nice it felt just to touch her. How much he wanted to hug her, kiss her. But the kids were only a room away, and Katie wasn't looking at him the same way anymore. Maybe if they talked, he could straighten this out and they could go back to where they were before. "Please stay."

She turned to the sink, her gaze on the dishes. "Okay.

But only for a few minutes after the kids go to bed. I have some things I have to do tonight."

Things that would bring her closer to returning to Atlanta? He didn't want to ask.

Either way, she was staying for now, and that was good enough for him.

"Sounds good." He couldn't stop a grin from swinging across his face. Whatever was bothering Katie they could clear up with a conversation, he was sure. Because he liked this woman—more than liked her—and didn't want her to slip away.

He started the water in the sink, but Katie stopped him. "I'll do the dishes. I'm sure you have some work to get caught up on," she said.

"Work can wait. I'll take you up on doing the dishes, because it's one of my least favorite chores, but I will take the opportunity to go watch Elsa for the thousandth time with my kids." Sam pressed a kiss to Katie's cheek, then headed for the living room.

He sank onto the sofa, and felt the world set itself to rights again when Henry and Libby curled under his arms. How long had it been since he had done this? Far too long, that was for sure. By the time the movie ended, Henry had fallen asleep and Libby was yawning. Sam hoisted Henry into his arms, then took Libby's hand. "Come on, Libby Bear, bedtime."

Libby nodded, too tired to mount her usual protest.

Sam paused in the kitchen, where Katie had stayed. She'd cleaned up from dinner and was doing something on her phone, probably answering emails. Accepting that job offer she'd mentioned? He hoped not, at least not until she heard him out tonight. "I'll be back down in ten minutes, tops."

"That's fine," she said.

He took the kids to bed, tucking Henry in first, then heading to Libby's room. She was already in her pajamas and under her covers. Sam sank onto her bed and smoothed the hair across her forehead. "Are you okay, Libby?"

She nodded. "I'm sorry I ran away, Daddy."

He'd never get tired of hearing that word again. Just hearing her say "Daddy" told him they'd come a long way in the last few days. "I'm just glad you're home. Next time you get upset, come talk to me, okay?"

Libby fiddled with the edge of her blanket. "Is it okay if I talk to Katie sometimes? Because she's a girl and sometimes..."

"It's girl stuff." He chuckled. "I understand."

Then he thought about how Katie was leaving soon. He debated telling Libby, then decided she had enough to deal with. Later, hopefully much later, he'd deal with that. "Good night, Libby Bear."

"Wait, Daddy. Can you read me a story?"

As long as she kept saying Daddy, he'd read every book on her shelf. He'd missed so much in the last year and a half and vowed not to miss a moment more.

Sam pulled out Libby's favorite book—the same one about the princess he had read a few nights ago—and sat back against Libby's headboard. This time, she curled onto his chest, and fell asleep before he got past page ten. He leaned down, tucked her under the covers, then pressed a kiss to her temple. "I love you, Libby Bear," he whispered. She smiled in her sleep, and Sam tiptoed out of the room, counting his blessings.

Katie had moved to the back deck while he was upstairs. He opened a bottle of wine, then came outside with two glasses, handing one to her.

"Thanks," she said.

He took a seat in the other Adirondack chair. Above them, the sky had turned purple as night began to take over the land. It was still warm out, with a light breeze that tickled the tops of the trees. "I should be thanking you," he said.

"For what? I lost your daughter today." She put up a hand when he started to speak. "And please don't apologize for getting mad at me. You were totally justified in that. I screwed up."

He took her hand in his. Her fingers were cold, and he rubbed the backs with his own. "You were human. There's nothing wrong with that. Heck, I lost Libby once in a supermarket. Wendy had just had Henry, so I told her I'd take the kids to the grocery store so she could get some rest. Henry was a handful, colicky, and I was trying to soothe him. Next thing I knew, I turned around and Libby was gone."

"Where did she go?"

"The toy aisle." Sam chuckled. "I should have known. I ran up and down all the other aisles, got the manager to call her name on the loudspeaker, and when we found her, she was sitting on the floor, playing with a Barbie doll. I felt like the worst parent in the world. I think maybe—" he paused "—maybe that's when I started to pull back, to be involved less. To work more. Wendy was such a fabulous mom, you know? I felt like all I was going to do was screw it up."

"Your kids love you, Sam. They don't expect perfection. They just want you to be there."

"You've been telling me that all along, but I haven't listened. I guess I was afraid..." He drew in a deep breath. "Afraid that I'd never be as good as their mother was. She really was a great mom. But I realized something today, when I was up in that castle at the playground with Libby. She didn't need me to do anything other than be there and listen and hold her when she cried." He drew in another breath and let it out again. He vowed that from this moment forward, things would be different. Never again would he forget what was important.

He thought of Libby curling into him, of her saying "Daddy" for the first time in months. Whatever it took, he wasn't going to lose that again. "I have to do a better job at balancing my career and being a good dad."

Katie took a sip of her wine and looked out over the lawn. "Trust me, you could be doing a lot worse. Your kids are happy and healthy. You are doing your best, and that's a lot better than the crappy job of parenting some people do."

"People like your mom." He thought of what Colton had said. Was that part of why Katie wanted to run? Because she was afraid of getting close to anyone again?

She hung her head and stared at the wine in her glass. From somewhere down the street, there was the sound of kids playing basketball. A horn beeping. A bird making one last call.

"Yeah, my mom," Katie said finally. "And when it mattered most, what happened? I was just as bad as she was."

"Are you talking about today? Like I said, Katie, that wasn't a mistake. You had no idea Libby was going to run off."

"I'm not talking about today." Katie pulled her hand out of his, then pushed off from the chair and got to her feet. She wrapped her arms around her waist and stood slightly to the right, her face averted from his. The crescent moon shone above her, like a halfhearted smile. "Listen, I know where a relationship with a guy like you ends. You told me yourself you want to get married and have more kids. I'm not the girl for that, so please, just stop trying to make this work."

He rose, leaving his wineglass on the arm of the chair. He came around in front of her, but still she wouldn't look at him. "And what makes you think you're not the right girl?" He leaned in closer, until only a breath separated them. Her eyes widened and her lips parted. He refused to let this woman go back to Georgia without a fight. "Because I think you're the right girl. I think you're very, very much the right girl, Katie."

Before she could pull away, he leaned in and kissed her. A sweet kiss at first, slow and easy, then her arms went around his neck, and his hands went to her waist and he pulled her close. Their kiss deepened, the heat building as quickly as it had before, and—

Katie jerked back and shook her head. "We can't do this, Sam. You're wrong about me. I'm not the right girl for you. Just let that whole idea go. Let *me* go."

"I can't." He took a step closer, then brushed a tendril of hair off her face. "I'm falling in love with you."

He hadn't realized that until this morning, until he'd finally stopped hiding behind the wall of work. The thing that kept him from being afraid of losing someone close to him again.

Katie's eyes widened. "You…you can't. Don't do this, Sam."

"I don't understand you. You kiss me, you make love to me, you fit in with my kids like adding cheese to chili." He grinned at the joke, but she didn't echo his smile. He took her hands in his, but they were cold again. "Why don't you think we're good together? Why don't you want the same thing as I do? Because I sure as hell thought you did."

"I do want it." She yanked her hands out of his and let out a gusty sigh. "I can't have it. I can't explain... I have to go."

She spun on her heel, but he stepped in front of her before she could escape. There was something Katie was leaving out, some missing piece to the equation. He hadn't been blind when he'd seen her light up around the kids or plan that beach adventure game or make love to him. That had all been real, and true, but now Katie was acting as if it had never happened. "Why are you not right for me? Tell me."

"Because...you want different things than I do." She glanced away from him, and he knew, deep in his gut, that for some reason Katie was lying. To him, to herself.

"You don't want to get married and have a family?"

"Once upon a time, I thought I did, but..."

"But what?" He put a hand to her cheek, searching her gaze. "Tell me, Katie."

"Why can't you let this go? I lost your daughter today. If anything proves I shouldn't be with you, it's that."

"Katie, you had an argument with Libby and she ran off. Kids do that. It's okay. Everyone's okay."

She shook her head. Tears filled her eyes. "Just let me go, Sam. Stop trying to make me into something I'm not."

"You're everything I want, Katie. Why can't you—"

"Because I lost the baby!" She tore away from him and stalked across the yard, coming to a stop in front of the large oak tree. A tire swing hung from its widest branch, drifting lazily in the breeze.

*Lost the baby?* He let those words roll around in his mind for a moment. They'd had sex only a few days ago and they'd used protection, so he knew she couldn't mean his child. He thought about what Colton had said, about how there had been events in Katie's recent past that had spurred her coming to Stone Gap. Was that part of it? "What do you mean, you lost the baby?"

The yard was quiet, with just the soft sound of crickets chirping and the whisper of a breeze in the trees. The rain had stopped and everything sparkled in the moonlight.

"Maybe if I tell you, you'll see why I'm so wrong for you, for this family." Her voice was hoarse, and tears welled in her eyes. "I got pregnant a few months ago. At the time, I was sure I didn't want to settle down, or have a family, because my mom was so terrible, you know? And I had always vowed I would never turn out like her, so I thought if I didn't have a family, I never could. But as I got used to the idea of being pregnant, I started to get excited about it. I started making plans, clearing out space for a nursery. Creating a future."

"What about the baby's father?"

She scoffed. "Turns out he wasn't interested in anything more permanent than a weekend. As soon as I told him I was pregnant, he was gone."

Bastard. Sam couldn't understand men who did that. Man enough to have sex, but not man enough to raise a child.

"But I was okay with that," Katie went on. "I wanted the baby and I was excited about it, but still scared, you know, that I wasn't ready. So..." She bit her lip and looked away for a minute, her gaze lingering on the darkness in the back of the yard. "So I worked. A lot. Extra hours, weekends, whatever I could do, to try to fatten up my savings so I'd be ready when the baby came."

He could understand pouring yourself into work to

avoid the memories, the things that hurt. He'd done it himself for so long. Too long.

"And then..." Her voice trailed off.

She didn't need to finish the sentence. He could see how much the memory hurt her. But as the tears welled again in her eyes, he put the pieces together. "You don't think working overtime caused that, do you? That you were at fault?"

"Maybe if I'd rested more and taken care of my body more..." She cursed and shook her head. The tears brimmed and spilled over her lashes, running in little rivers down her cheeks. "I woke up one morning and it was over. I knew it, the second I felt the pain. And it was *my* fault. I don't care what the doctor said, I was the reason the baby..." She swiped at her tears. "The reason I couldn't do the one thing that millions of women do every year."

His heart broke for her, for this woman who loved so much, and yet couldn't forgive herself. "Katie, miscarriages happen all the time. It doesn't mean it was your fault."

"Don't you understand? I can't be a mother. I can't keep track of your kid, and I can't even hold on to my own." She spun away from him, standing tall and cold in the dark. "So just let me go, Sam."

"I can't. Because I already love you." The minute he said the words, he knew they were true. He loved the way she smiled, the way she talked to his kids, the way she made every burden he had seem easier with her beside him.

She stood there, her back to him, for a long moment. "Please don't say that. You're not listening to me. I... I should go."

He came up in front of her and waited until she raised

her gaze to his. "You're running away because you're scared. I know, because I did it myself for years with my job. I ran away from my family because I was scared I was not going to be half the parent my wife was. I ran away because it was easier than facing that fear and being here. It almost cost me my relationship with my kids." He looped a finger under the stubborn lock of hair that had fallen across Katie's forehead again, and tucked it behind her ear. "You're scared, too. I get that. But don't let that fear ruin your life."

"I'm not," she said, and her voice caught on a sob. "I'm trying not to let it ruin yours."

Then she spun on her heel and left. Sam stood in his backyard while the moon moved across the sky and the world went to sleep. He stood there, thinking if he stayed long enough, his heart would stop aching.

He was wrong.

## Chapter Fifteen

"If I tell you that you are an idiot, are you going to listen to me?" Colton said.

Katie looked up to see Colton grinning at her.

"And I say that with love," he added, "just in case you were wondering."

She was sitting across from her brother in a corner booth and picking at a breakfast she didn't really want. She'd asked to meet him this morning so she could have a chance to say goodbye before she hit the road. "I'm not an idiot. I'm just making the smartest choice for me and Sam."

Her brother took a bite of toast, chewed and swallowed. "Uh-huh. Sounds to me like you're running away."

"Sam said the same thing." She shook her head and pushed the coffee in front of her to the side. What was with the men in her life? Didn't they understand she wasn't running away? She was just making a smart decision. For her career, for her apartment. For all the things she could depend on, that didn't come with emotional attachments. Getting back to those ordered lines. "I have to go back to Atlanta. I need to find a job, pay my bills, feed the alley cat."

"You don't have an alley cat."

"I'll find one." Adopt one, rescue one, borrow one. Something to take her mind off how much it had hurt to pack her bags this morning. Her car was just outside the Good Eatin' Café, and before she knew it, she'd be behind the wheel and driving home.

Except Atlanta didn't seem like home. It never really had. This quirky little town with a restaurant owner who remembered her name and an inn owner who'd teared up when she said she was checking out this morning—this was what felt like home. Heck, it had felt like home from the minute she'd arrived.

For a second, she considered staying in Stone Gap. After all, there were accounting jobs here, too. She could surely find one or even open her own office. Staying here would mean seeing Henry, Libby, and most of all, Sam.

She couldn't do that. Not without dissolving into a puddle of tears every time.

Hence the need for an alley cat.

"So why don't you stay?" Colton asked, as if reading her mind. "Because the one thing you've never really done, Piglet, is stay."

"I do, too. I have an apartment in Atlanta."

"And have you done anything permanent at your place?" Colton arched a brow and leaned forward. "Like plant a garden or buy a desk?"

"I live in an apartment, Colton. I can't plant a garden. And the firm provided me with a desk. I didn't need to buy one."

"Which means when you were not fired–fired, you could pack everything you owned into a cardboard box and walk out the door." Colton took another bite of toast.

"Well, yeah, but I don't see—"

"And if your apartment was to burn down tomorrow, would you be upset about losing anything inside there?"

"Well, I have a photo album from when we were kids, but really, it's all replaceable "

"And leavable."

She laughed. "I don't think that's a word."

"My point is that you don't even have things that tie you down, never mind people or places. You can leave at any time—or rather, you can run away at any time. In the two weeks you were here, you made connections. You made friends. You made memories. And if you ask me—" he leaned back in his seat and picked up a second piece of toast "—you're having a hell of a hard time running away from those, because you can't pack any of that in a cardboard box." Colton popped the toast in his mouth and gave her a told-you-so nod.

"That's not it. That's crazy. I'm..." Her voice trailed off as she thought about what her brother had said. There was no one in Atlanta she was rushing to get back to see. She had friends, yes, but most of them were people she joined for dinner after work. There was no one in her contacts list that she would call for a pizza and movie night. No one she wanted to explore an old house with. No one she wanted to go fishing with or search for treasures in the sand with.

No one except for Sam.

"You can tell me I'm right anytime you want." Colton gave her a cheesy grin.

"I'm not saying you're right…" She realigned her fork and knife beside the plate. "Just that you might… *might* have a point."

"Then why are you still sitting here with me?"

"We're having breakfast."

Colton reached over, grabbed her plate, forked up the last of her eggs, then drained her coffee. "There. Now we're done."

Katie laughed. "Has anyone ever told you that you're a pain in the ass?"

"You. Every day of my life." He got to his feet and pressed a kiss to her forehead. "I love you, sis. Now get the hell out of here."

"And go where?"

"The mall on Route 104. Sam has an appointment to meet an interested client there at 10:00 a.m."

"Oh, I shouldn't interrupt him if he's…" She glanced at her brother's face. She recognized that meddling look. She couldn't be mad, because she knew Colton always had the best of intentions, like when he'd gone up to the playground bully when she was in third grade and told him to stop stealing his sister's lunch money. Colton was always going to look after Katie's best interests, even when she didn't need him to. "You?"

"Me? I'm not interested in the real estate Sam's offering. But I bet you are." He shooed her toward the door and tossed a twenty dollar bill on the table. "Now hurry up, because after you're done falling in love with Sam—"

"Who said I was falling in love with Sam?"

"Your goofy grin and googly eyes whenever I talk about him. As I was saying, after you are done falling in love with Sam, I'd love to invite you to dinner at my fiancée's house. Because if you're going to be moving here, you should get to know your sister-in-law." Then he leaned in just as Katie was heading out the door. "And bonus, Rachel's a wedding planner. I have a feeling that might come in handy one day soon."

Sam paced the two-thousand-square-foot space that he'd stood in just days earlier with Ginny and Bernard. They were still debating between this space and the one next door, but had put earnest money on both, just in case. With that deal, it put the mall occupancy at 90 percent—making Hank very, very happy with his new Realtor. Only one more space to fill and Sam would have accomplished his goal. If this next client worked out, that was.

His ten o'clock was running late. He'd called the office and asked for more information, but the receptionist said she didn't have any details about who was meeting him, or have a call-back number. Weird, but he'd met eccentric investors who did that kind of thing from time to time. He just hoped the meeting wouldn't be a complete waste of his time.

He had called Katie and texted her several times after she'd left his house last night, but she hadn't responded. For all he knew, she was already on the road back to Atlanta.

It was Tuesday, and Della had agreed to watch his kids this week until he found a new nanny. If he could tie everything up with the properties he was showing by Friday morning, then he could pick the kids up after Libby got out of school and take a road trip to Georgia. The woman he had made love to, the woman he had laughed with on the beach, that woman was the one he loved—and the same one that he was sure was scared to settle down.

She'd been wounded by the loss of her baby, and he could understand why she would see that as somehow her fault. But she was wrong, and he intended to spend as much time as it took to show her that.

The door to the shop opened and Sam pivoted around. His heart leaped into his throat and he had to blink to be sure he wasn't seeing things. "Katie."

"Hi." She gave him a shy smile, then stepped inside. The door shut again with a soft whoosh. "Can we talk?"

"Sure. But I have an appointment—" He stopped talking when he noticed her smile widen. "*You're* the appointment?"

She put out her arms and shrugged. "Blame Colton, the closet matchmaker."

Sam laughed. "Your brother's become a big romantic since he met Rachel."

"Tell me about it. He's practically a walking Nicholas Sparks novel now, except with a happy ending." She walked around the room, looking up at the tall ceilings with their exposed pipes and oversize pendant lights. She was wearing jeans today, with little heeled boots and a short-sleeved blue sweater. She looked incredible and beautiful, and it took everything he had not to sweep her into his arms. "So, if someone were interested in renting this place, what would it have to offer?"

"You mean, someone who is interested in staying in Stone Gap and maybe opening up an office?" He grinned, then shifted into business mode when she didn't reply. Okay, so that joke went flat. Best to focus on business. "It's a standard triple-net lease, utilities included. The anchor store is opening in three weeks, which should drive a lot of traffic to this end of the mall. The entire space is customizable to your needs and there's a loading dock right out back."

"Sounds…promising." She'd stopped walking and now stood in the center of the room.

Sam crossed to her and tried to read Katie's mind. She was an enigma right now. He couldn't decide if she was seriously interested in the space, making small talk or speaking in some kind of code about them. He opted for the third possibility and hoped he wasn't going to look like a fool in the end. "It is a promising deal," he said. "It has a lot to offer, but you have to move quickly. There's more than one interested party."

"There is?"

He nodded. "They've already made an offer. They want it to be a long-term deal, even though it's really risky, because it's a brand-new venture for them."

The room was wide and empty, almost symbolic in its blankness. It could be a new beginning—for a business owner, for a shop operator or for him and Katie. He held his breath, waiting, not yet ready to bank on anything.

"What made them lock into a long-term deal?" Katie asked.

"They're either fools or optimists," he said. "I prefer to go with the optimists' option."

She laughed softly. "And I'm thinking they're fools. If it's a new venture and you don't have the data to back up your decision, better to not take the risk. Especially not a long-term risk."

Were they talking about the commercial space or about them? "Sometimes the best option is just to take the leap."

She cocked her head and studied him. "But what if you don't know what's on the other side?"

"None of us know what's on the other side, Katie." He took her hand in his. She didn't pull away. Hope bloomed in his chest. He'd spent too many months stuck in thick mud, not moving forward or backward.

He thought of the picture of Wendy that Libby had been holding in the castle. His wife had always been one to live every day with gusto, because she'd said she was never sure what tomorrow would bring. She wouldn't want him to stay in the mud—she would want him to move forward, to grab today, because tomorrow could bring something unexpected. The last bits of his guilt ebbed, and he took a step closer to Katie. To a new future. "Life is short, Katie. That's one thing I have learned in spades in the last year and a half. You need to take the risk."

"But what if I screw up?" Her grip tightened on his, and her face creased with worry. "In accounting, all the numbers add up, even out. That's not how it is with love, with kids. With a family."

He remembered feeling that way before his kids were born, and then letting that fear get in his way after the day Libby got away from him in the grocery store. He thought of how many things had changed in the last few days, and how the children he loved had come back around. Things were different now, and for the first time in a long time, he could see brightness on the horizon. Katie had been the one to foster those changes, to open his heart again. He wished she could see that. "Nothing is ever gonna line up perfectly with kids, with the people you love. But that's what makes it so great. Life is messy and complicated, but all you have to do is love each other, and it'll all be okay."

It was the lesson he had finally understood sitting in the turret of the playground castle. Libby just needed him to love her, to be there, to set her world to rights again.

Katie turned away and started walking the perimeter of the room again. Putting distance between them, every time they got close. "This space has good bones," she said. "And with a little renovation, it could be perfect. It's worth it, though, isn't it? To do the work?"

"Yes, it is. Then you can get what you really want." He sighed. She really was just talking about the rental space. He tried to mask his disappointment, but it sat like a stone in his gut. "We can work with whatever renovation timeline you have. Though you might want to look at one of the other two properties I still have available. Like I said, this one has an offer on it already."

She pivoted back toward him. "I don't want any other properties. I want this one."

"I can't..." He took two steps closer and saw the mischief lurking in her eyes. Again, his heart leaped, held, cautious. "You want this one?"

She put a hand on his chest and smiled up at him. "This one right here. And no other."

"But what about Atlanta and your job?"

"They need accountants here. In fact, I called the firm in downtown Stone Gap on my way over and I have an interview later this afternoon." She looked scared and excited all at once. "I don't have a job offer or a plan, so there are no guarantees, but it's a step. And if a job with another firm doesn't work out, I can always go out on my own."

"That's great." He tried to work up some enthusiasm. She hadn't mentioned him or if they had any kind of future together. "So...you're thinking about staying in Stone Gap?"

"I'd like to make it a permanent move. My very wise and bossy brother lives here, and my soon-to-be sister-in-law. I want to be the terrible auntie who spoils their kids rotten."

Again, no mention of him. It was almost more painful to stand here. For a second there, Sam had thought she was talking about wanting him, wanting them. But now… "That sounds great. I bet Colton will be happy."

"And what about you?"

"What about me?"

"Would you be happy if I stayed in Stone Gap and spoiled Colton's kids?" she said.

"First of all, I am totally on board with spoiling Colton's kids as long as it involves a drum set to make up for the bongos he bought my kids for Christmas." Sam closed the gap between them and settled his hands on her waist. She didn't back away, and the hope in his chest grew. "Secondly, nothing would make me happier than for you to live permanently in Stone Gap. If… if we were together."

Her gaze softened, and a smile curved across her face. "I'm tired of running away, Sam. I want…a life I can depend on. A life I build and take the time to enjoy."

He drew her to him, and murmured against the soft locks of her hair, "Then stop running, Katie."

"I'm still scared."

He pressed his forehead to hers. Their eyes met, held. "Me, too. But I don't want to put my life on hold anymore because of what might happen. I want to live in the present."

"Me, too." Katie's smile widened, and Sam thought he would love nothing more than to see that smile every day of his life. "I love you, Sam Millwright."

She loved him? The words lifted his heart, filled him with joy. "I love you, too, Katie, even if you are completely overqualified to be with me."

"Completely overqualified?"

"I don't think you're right for the nanny job," he said, and paused a beat when confusion filled her gaze. "I think you should be my wife."

Katie's eyes widened. "But what if I can't have any more children? What if—"

He placed a finger on her lips. "That's not a requirement for being my wife, Katie. I want you, and the magic you've brought back to my life, to my kids' lives. I want to laugh with you and eat pizza with you and find treasures on the beach with you. For the rest of my life."

"I already found the best treasure," she said. "Right here." Katie leaned into his chest, listened to his heart beat. Sam held her tight, in an empty space that would someday hold someone else's future, and for the first time in her life, Katie stayed exactly where she was, and began to put down roots.

# *Epilogue*

*Eighteen months later*

Bright balloons waved in the slight breeze, while the sound of children's laughter rang like bells across the lawn. Stone Gap Lake sparkled in the spring sunlight, the water beckoning, even if it was still too cold to swim.

The house Sam had bought years ago was finally restored, after months of hard work by Savannah Barlow and her crew. Today was the official housewarming, now that Sam, Katie, Libby and Henry were all settled in. There were still some pictures to hang, some pillows to fluff, but overall, the house was a home. The kids loved the lake in their backyard, the room for the new swing set Sam had installed, and the tree house he'd begun constructing last weekend. All of the Barlow boys had been here to help with that one, though it seemed the men had spent more time ribbing each other than actually building. It didn't matter. Katie had loved looking out the kitchen window and seeing the big family that she'd always wanted, expanding by the minute.

Now, Katie lowered herself into a chair and let out a long breath. Her back ached, no matter how often Sam rubbed the sore spot at the base of her spine. She watched Della Barlow hand out cookies to Libby, Henry and Maddy, her face filled with joy at the sight of her grandchildren. She'd officially declared herself Libby and Henry's grandmother, even if the familial link was several times removed. Katie didn't mind. It was nice to be wrapped in the warm embrace of the Barlow family, sort of like cocooning under blankets on a cold winter's night.

"Here you go," Sam said as he handed her a plate and took a seat in the Adirondack chair beside her. "Though I have no idea how you're eating that."

She laughed. "Don't blame me for the menu. Blame the baby." The final stages of her pregnancy had left her with a lot of weird cravings, including hot dogs topped with potato chips and mustard. Not to mention the pickle and apple slices on the side.

Sam's hand slid across her belly with a soft, slow, proud swirl. The sun glinted off the gold in his ring. "I can't wait till we finally get to meet him."

"Her," Katie gently corrected as the baby let out a gentle kick. "I think it's a girl."

"And I'm betting on boy." He grinned. "Either way, we'll know in a week."

For months after she saw the positive result on the pregnancy test, Katie had held her breath, too afraid to hope. Then as the first trimester stretched into the second, and then the third, she'd begun to plan, to paint the nursery with Sam, to fill a crib with stuffed animals (and even a bear that Libby and Henry had picked out for their new sibling). Now, with only a few days to go, Katie was filled with nervous anticipation. Sam was ecstatic, as were the kids. It was a bright new beginning for all of them, a perfect start that had begun the day she'd said "I do" to Sam on this very lawn last year.

Her hand covered his and their fingers interlaced. "It's a first baby. It might be late."

Sam leaned in and kissed her. He pressed his forehead to hers and met her gaze. "It'll be worth the wait."

"Quit kissing my sister." Colton grinned at the two of them. His wife, Rachel, was holding his hand, looking up at Colton like the sun rose in his face. They still had that just-married look, fourteen months after their own wedding. There were days when Katie could hardly believe she'd first come to Stone Gap a year and a half ago. So much had changed in that time.

"You do know where that kissing business leads, don't you?" Colton added.

Katie laughed and gave her belly a pat. "I do indeed. And if I'm not mistaken, so do you."

Rachel blushed and a hand strayed to her abdomen, the kind of unconscious gesture of a woman with a new life inside her. "How did you know? We just found out ourselves a few days ago."

"This family is having a baby boom," Sam said. "It only seemed right that you guys would be next."

Meri Barlow came over to them, with Jack right beside her. Jack had a sleepy six-month-old on his shoulder, a little blonde girl who looked as beautiful as her mother. "As much as I'd love to let Sam take credit for some kind of familial ESP, I might have let the news slip," Meri said, then turned to her sister-in-law. "You kinda told me yourself, Rachel, when you asked if I still had Liz's newborn clothes."

Rachel's face reddened even more. "I said I was asking for a friend."

The Barlows and the Millwrights laughed. "Yeah,

we all know that's code for asking for yourself," Jack said. "Either way, I'm glad to see you and Colton joining the party."

Luke and Peyton came strolling over, hand in hand. Luke clapped a hand on his brother's back. "What are the girls roping you into now, Colton?"

"The one thing you and Mac haven't been roped into yet," Colton said. "Kids."

"I already have one of those, you know. If I want more, I can borrow from a wide selection of Barlow youngsters." Luke drew Peyton into his arms and pressed a kiss to her temple. His arm looped around her waist and his voice lowered when he spoke again. "Though I don't think I'd mind adding one or two to our mix."

Peyton's eyes widened and a smile took over her face. "Is that you saying you want to have a baby?"

"It is." Luke's love for his wife showed in his eyes, his voice. They were rarely apart, even when Luke was working at the family garage. Most days, Peyton and Maddy stopped by there to eat lunch or share an early dinner with Luke. He tore his gaze away from her, then shouted over his head at Mac, who was helping Savannah slice a watermelon. "What do you say, Mac? Want to see who can have a son first?"

Mac arched a brow. "Are you seriously challenging me to an offspring challenge?"

"Somebody's got to make you finish settling down." Luke grinned. Mac had been the last of them to get married. He and Savannah had had a simple affair in Della and Bobby's backyard just three months ago.

"If you all would quit keeping my wife so busy with renovation projects, maybe we could find time to have kids."

Savannah swatted at him. "Shush. I love doing this work."

"And you do it well, sweetheart," Mac said softly, then kissed her. As much as the other men teased Mac, Katie could see every one of the Barlow family members were glad to see so much happiness among the brothers.

Della came up the little hill with the nearly empty tray of cookies still in her hand. "Did I just hear something about more grandchildren?" When she saw Rachel and Colton's twin smiles and shy nods of yes, Della let out a whoop, handed off the cookies to Luke, then grabbed the two of them in an excited hug.

Life was good, Katie thought, as she watched her children running along the edge of the lake with Bandit, and treasured the warmth of her husband's hand in hers. How things had changed in the space of time since she first arrived in Stone Gap, a town she couldn't imagine ever leaving. Especially not since she'd put down roots, and watched them grow into a family tree.

Even though she'd had an offer from the Stone Gap accounting firm, Katie had opened a little accounting practice out of the house, using what would have been the parlor as a home office. She worked part-time, which left her enough time to be with the kids when they got home from school, and spend lots of time with Sam, going on family scavenger hunts along the lakeshore. The new mall project that Sam had worked on filling had gone so well that the developers had asked him to help them fill another mall being built thirty miles outside of Stone Gap. He worked hard, but he'd stuck to his promise to spend more time with his family and not let work bleed over into that precious personal time. He'd already planned for a two-week vacation for after the baby came. It'd be nice to have him around more often. Very nice.

"I hear Savannah designed one hell of a garage for

you, Sam," Jack said. "Want to take us guys on a tour so we can drool over it?"

"Yeah, and we'll take the cookies for sustenance since we might be in there awhile, making up our own wish lists for Christmas." Luke swiped the rest of them into his palm, then handed the tray back to his mother.

Sam chuckled, then got to his feet. He bent down toward Katie again. "Are you going to be okay if I leave you for a bit?"

She laughed and gave him a nod. "Yes, worrywart, I will be. We've got a week, remember? And besides, I'm not going anywhere."

Love warmed Sam's brown eyes. "I'm never going to get tired of hearing you say that," he whispered, then gave her a kiss before heading off with the Barlow brothers. The men joked and laughed as they walked away, teasing Sam about the "man cave" Savannah had built in one of the garage bays.

Della took a seat beside Katie and gave her a quick hug. "I'm so glad you came to town and joined our crazy clan," she said.

"Even if I'm barely related?"

Della took Katie's hand in hers and gave it a squeeze. "You've been family since the day you arrived at the Stone Gap Inn, Katie."

The words warmed Katie, and filled her heart. The family she had found—Sam, Libby, Henry, the Barlows—had welcomed her and Colton with open arms. She could feel her life becoming full and complete, becoming the world she had never dared to dream existed when she was little and staring at those cracks in the ceiling.

A low, heavy pain rippled across her abdomen, and Katie let out a little gasp. She'd had several of those throughout the day, and kept thinking they were just more Braxton Hicks contractions. But this one was different, stronger somehow, and Katie's instincts told her this first baby wasn't going to be late, after all.

Katie looked over at Della. "I think you need to go get Sam."

Della's gaze dropped to Katie's belly, then back up to her face. "It's time?"

Katie nodded, and felt tears of joy spring to her eyes. She may have taken almost three decades to get here, to this town, to this man, to the family she'd dreamed of, but the wait, as Sam had said, had been worth it. "It's time."

\* \* \* \* \*

*Don't miss the previous books in*

New York Times *Bestselling Author Shirley Jump's*
THE BARLOW BROTHERS *series*
*for Mills & Boon Cherish*

*THE HOMECOMING QUEEN GETS HER MAN*

*THE INSTANT FAMILY MAN*

*THE TYCOON'S PROPOSAL*

*and*

*THE FIREFIGHTER'S FAMILY SECRET*

*Available wherever Mills & Boon books
and ebooks are sold.*

# MILLS & BOON®

## *Cherish*™

**EXPERIENCE THE ULTIMATE RUSH OF FALLING IN LOVE**

## A sneak peek at next month's titles...

### In stores from 12th January 2017:

- **The Sheikh's Convenient Princess** – Liz Fielding *and* **His Pregnant Courthouse Bride** – Rachel Lee
- **The Billionaire of Coral Bay** – Nikki Logan *and* **Baby Talk & Wedding Bells** – Brenda Harlen

### In stores from 26th January 2017:

- **Her First-Date Honeymoon** – Katrina Cudmore *and* **Falling for the Rebound Bride** – Karen Templeton
- **The Unforgettable Spanish Tycoon** – Meg Maxwell *and* **Her Sweetest Fortune** – Stella Bagwell

# MILLS & BOON®

## EXCLUSIVE EXTRACT

Sheikh Ibrahim al-Ansari must find a bride,
and quickly… Thankfully he has the perfect
convenient princess in mind—his new assistant,
Ruby Dance!

*Read on for a sneak preview of*
**THE SHEIKH'S CONVENIENT PRINCESS**
by Liz Fielding

'Can I ask if you are in any kind of relationship?' he
persisted.

'Relationship?'

'You are on your own—you have no ties?'

He was beginning to spook her and must have realised
it because he said, 'I have a proposition for you, Ruby,
but if you have personal commitments…' He shook his
head as if he wasn't sure what he was doing.

'If you're going to offer me a package too good to
refuse after a couple of hours I should warn you that it
took Jude Radcliffe the best part of a year to get to that
point and I still turned him down.'

'I don't have the luxury of time,' he said, 'and the
position I'm offering is made for a temp.'

'I'm listening.'

'Since you have done your research, you know that
I was disinherited five years ago.'

She nodded. She thought it rather harsh for a one-off

incident but the media loved the fall of a hero and had gone into a bit of a feeding frenzy.

'This morning I received a summons from my father to present myself at his birthday majlis.'

'You can go home?'

'If only it were that simple. A situation exists which means that I can only return to Umm al Basr if I'm accompanied by a wife.'

She ignored the slight sinking feeling in her stomach. Obviously a multimillionaire who looked like the statue of a Greek god—albeit one who'd suffered a bit of wear and tear—would have someone ready and willing to step up to the plate.

'That's rather short notice. Obviously, I'll do whatever I can to arrange things, but I don't know a lot about the law in—'

'The marriage can take place tomorrow. My question is, under the terms of your open-ended brief encompassing "whatever is necessary", are you prepared to take on the role?'

*Don't miss*
THE SHEIKH'S CONVENIENT PRINCESS
By Liz Fielding

Available February 2017
www.millsandboon.co.uk

# Give a 12 month subscription to a friend today!

## Call Customer Services
### 0844 844 1358*

## or visit
### millsandboon.co.uk/subscriptions